THE VIOLIN'S CURSE

Copyright © 2025

All rights are reserved, and no part of this publication may be reproduced, distributed, or transmitted in any manner, whether through photocopying, recording, or any other electronic or mechanical methods, without the explicit prior written permission of the publisher. This restriction applies to any form or means of reproduction or distribution.

Exceptions to this rule include brief quotations that may be incorporated into critical reviews, as well as certain other noncommercial uses that are allowed by copyright law. Any such usage must adhere to the specified conditions and permissions outlined by the copyright holder.

Book Design by HmdPublishing

CONTENTS

PROLOGUE

The shop stood quietly on the edge of the cobblestone street, its windows darkened by age and dust, save for a small glass display near the entrance. Inside, Theo Callahan worked in silence, the muted hum of the city beyond barely reaching him. His hands moved with practiced precision, polishing the dark wood of a violin whose intricate carvings seemed to shimmer under the workbench lamp.

It was no ordinary instrument. The violin exuded an unsettling presence as though it were alive in its stillness. A faint hum vibrated in the air, a sound too soft to be heard yet impossible to ignore. Its surface bore an inscription, E.H., 1867, etched faintly into the wood, a detail nearly erased by time but still legible to those who dared to look.

Theo carefully set the violin down, his fingers lingering on its curves as a sense of unease coiled in his chest. He knew better than to dismiss what the instrument carried. It wasn't just an antique, and it wasn't merely valuable; it was a piece of something vast that reached far beyond his understanding, something...darker.

Suddenly, the air shifted. At first, it was as subtle as a faint ripple across still water; then, the warmth of the shop faded away, replaced by a cold so sharp it bit at his skin.

Theo froze, his breath escaping in visible clouds that hung motionless in the chilled air. For a moment, it was as though the shop held its breath, time folding in on itself, leaving only... silence.

His gaze dropped to the violin, its polished surface gleaming unnaturally. The hum had grown louder, vibrating through the stillness like the whisper of a melody not meant to be heard.

Then, a faint echo, a sound that wasn't his own, brushed the edges of his hearing. A low, guttural note that twisted through the cold air like a warning.

Theo's eyes flicked toward the door, half-expecting someone to step inside. However, the doorway remained empty, the city beyond untouched by the unease within the shop. His attention returned to the violin, now silent but no less foreboding.

He exhaled slowly, the chill retreating but the tension lingering. Whatever emotions or stories this violin held were far from complete. He was sure of that.

There were objects in this world that carried more than history, objects that held stories waiting to be played out, no matter the cost. And some stories were better left unfinished.

Chapter 1

THE VIOLIN IN THE WINDOW

The sun was just beginning to dip behind the horizon, painting the train station in warm hues of orange and gold. Olivia Hart tightened the grip on her violin, the smooth wood comforting against her calloused fingers. The familiar screech of the trains and the hum of commuters filled the air, creating a symphony of chaos that oddly soothed her. This was her sanctuary, her escape.

She drew the bow across the strings, the melody soft at first, then swelling into something richer, more poignant. The music carried through the platform, slowing hurried steps and drawing curious glances. At her feet, a few coins clinked into the open case, but Olivia barely noticed. For a moment, she wasn't in the middle of a bustling London station; she was somewhere far away... lost in the sound.

The applause at the end of her song jolted her back to reality. Olivia glanced up and offered a faint smile to a small group of listeners before hurriedly packing her violin. Busking wasn't about the attention; it was about the music, a connection to something she couldn't quite name but felt deep in her soul.

As she slung the case over her shoulder and exited the station, a glint in a nearby shop window caught her eye. She stopped, narrowing her gaze at the display.

It was a violin, but not just any violin. Its dark, glossy surface seemed to absorb the fading sunlight, and intricate carvings traced the edges of its body. It was beautiful, haunting even, and something about it made Olivia's chest tighten. She stepped closer, pressing a hand against the glass.

"Looking for something in particular?"

The voice startled her. She turned to see a man standing in the shop's doorway, his arms crossed over a plain button-up shirt. His sharp jawline and dark hair gave him an air of quiet intensity, but it was his gray and piercing eyes that held her attention.

"I… no," Olivia stammered, stepping back. "I was just…"

"Admiring the violin," he finished for her, a hint of a smirk tugging at his lips. He turned and walked into the shop, leaving the door ajar. "You can come in if you'd like."

Olivia hesitated. She wasn't accustomed to wandering into antique shops, but something about the violin drew her in like certain melodies did when she first heard them. Taking a deep breath, she stepped inside.

The shop was a labyrinth of forgotten treasures, with dusty shelves filled with books, brass instruments, and trinkets that seemed to be plucked from another era. The violin rested on a small stand near the counter, and it was even more striking up close.

"Beautiful, isn't it?" the man said, appearing behind the counter.

Olivia nodded, unsure of what to say.

"Do you play?" he asked, his tone casual but curious.

"Yes," she replied. "I teach music, but… I play for myself sometimes."

He tilted his head. "A performer who doesn't perform. That's unusual."

Olivia bristled. "I didn't say I was a performer."

"No," he said, his smirk returning. "But you carry yourself like one. You play here often, don't you? At the station?"

Olivia frowned. "Have you been watching me?"

"Not intentionally," he said with a shrug. "You're hard to miss."

She wasn't sure if that was a compliment or an insult, but before she could respond, he gestured to the violin. "It's not for sale, by the way. Just in case you were wondering."

"I wasn't," Olivia lied. She took a step closer, her fingers itching to touch it. "Why isn't it for sale?"

The man hesitated, his expression softening. "It's... special. Let's just leave it at that."

Olivia wasn't satisfied with his answer, but she didn't press. Instead, she reached out, her fingers hovering over the violin's polished surface. A strange sensation washed over her, a mix of warmth and cold, like the moment before a storm. She pulled her hand back, startled.

"You felt it, didn't you?" the man asked quietly.

Olivia looked up at him, her heart pounding. "Felt what?"

He didn't answer right away. Instead, he studied her for a long moment before extending a hand. "Theo Callahan."

She shook it hesitantly. "Olivia Hart."

"Well, Olivia," Theo said, leaning against the counter, "if you're interested in that violin, we might have more to talk about than I thought."

His words hung in the air, and Olivia found herself unable to look away from the instrument. There was something about it, something that seemed to hum beneath the surface, pulling at her in a way she couldn't quite define.

Olivia lingered in the shop, her gaze fixed on the violin as Theo watched her with quiet curiosity. She couldn't explain its pull on her; it was more than mere fascination. It was a whisper, a thread that seemed to wind its way into her chest, tugging at memories she hadn't revisited in years.

"You're not going to pick it up?" Theo asked, pulling her attention back. His tone was casual, but his sharp gaze suggested he didn't miss much.

Olivia shook her head. "I... I don't know. It feels... strange."

Theo raised an eyebrow, clearly intrigued. "Strange how?"

"I don't know," she admitted. "It's like…" She trailed off, unwilling to sound ridiculous. "Never mind."

Theo leaned back against the counter, folding his arms. "You're not the first to say that about this violin."

Olivia looked at him sharply. "What do you mean?"

He hesitated for a moment as though deciding how much to tell her. "It's been in my shop for years. I've received good offers, yet I've never sold it. Anyone who plays it always says the same thing: it feels alive.."

Alive. The word sent a shiver down her spine. She glanced at the violin again, its dark, gleaming surface catching the light.

Her fingers twitched with the urge to play it, but she resisted. Instead, she stepped back, crossing her arms tightly over her chest. "I should go."

"Wait," Theo said. He grabbed a card from the counter and handed it to her. "If you change your mind, come back. I think you and that violin have something to work out."

Olivia frowned but took the card. It was simple, with only his name, the shop's name, Callahan Antiques, and the address. Without another word, she turned and left, the bell jingling softly behind her.

Outside, the crisp evening air bit at her skin. The streets were slick with rain from earlier, and the faint hum of the city surrounded her as she walked back toward her apartment. Her mind, however, was still in the shop, turning over Theo's words and the strange pull of the violin.

She let out a shaky breath and tightened her grip on the strap of her violin case. Music had always been her anchor, her lifeline. It wasn't just a hobby; it was a thread woven through her childhood, a bond that connected her to her father. She could still vividly remember those evenings when the sound of his playing filled their home like a living presence, wrapping around her like a warm embrace.

Her father had been a gentleman with warm brown eyes and a deep laugh that echoed through their small home. He wasn't just a violinist; he played with a passion that seemed to transcend the instrument. Olivia used to sit cross-legged on the worn rug in their living room, her wide eyes fixed on his hands as they danced over the strings with practiced grace.

"Music isn't just sound, Liv," he used to say, his voice soft but firm. "It's a story. Every note and rest is a piece of who you are. Do you feel it?"

She'd nodded, wide-eyed and eager, though she hadn't fully understood what he meant back then. But now, years later, his words resonated deeply. Music was the one place where she felt whole, where she could lose herself and still feel grounded.

Her father had taught her to play when she was seven, his hands guiding hers as she struggled with the bow. By the time she was ten, they were playing duets, her laughter filling the room whenever she stumbled over a note.

And then, one day, he was gone.

It had been fifteen years, but the memory of his disappearance still lingered like a dissonant chord in her mind. One day, he'd been there, promising to take her to Ireland to see the cliffs he loved so much. The next, he was simply… gone. No explanation, no closure. Just an empty house and her mother's tears.

Back in the present, Olivia blinked away the memory as she reached her apartment. She let herself in, her small flat silent except for the hum of the radiator. She placed her violin case on the table and sank into the couch, her head resting against the worn fabric.

Why couldn't she stop thinking about that violin?

Her own instrument sat untouched, its familiar shape suddenly feeling foreign. The violin in Theo's shop had stirred something in her, something she couldn't explain. She felt like a thread was pulling her toward it, unraveling memories and emotions she wasn't ready to face.

Unable to stop herself, Olivia pulled out her phone and opened a search engine. She typed in the shop's name: Callahan Antiques. The reviews were sparse, but one caught her eye.

"The violins here are special. Almost like they have their own stories. One in particular gave me chills, it felt like it was playing me, not the other way around. If you love music, you have to see it."

Olivia's fingers hovered over the screen. Her heart was pounding again, just like it had in the shop. She closed the browser and leaned back, staring at the ceiling.

She didn't believe in fate, but something about that violin felt inevitable. And the more she tried to ignore it, the louder its silent call became.

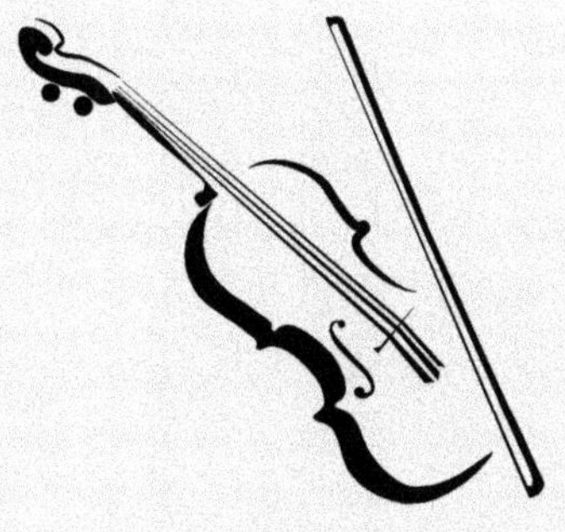

Chapter 2

THE HAUNTING NOTE

The following day, Olivia sat at her small kitchen table, staring at her violin. The sunlight streaming through the window glinted off its smooth surface, but her thoughts were elsewhere, back in Theo's shop with that violin. She had dreamed of it all night, its dark wood gleaming in the faint light, its strings vibrating with a melody she couldn't quite place.

She pressed her palms to her temples, trying to shake off the lingering unease. It was just a violin, she told herself. Beautiful, yes, but still just an instrument. And yet, when she closed her eyes, she could almost hear its song, a low, haunting note that seemed to vibrate in her chest.

Her phone buzzed, breaking her trance. She reached for it, grateful for the distraction, and saw a text from Sarah, her best friend since college.

Sarah: You're still coming tonight, right?

Olivia groaned. She had completely forgotten Sarah's dinner party, an annual tradition she reluctantly attended. It was supposed to be fun—good food, wine, catching up—but Olivia rarely felt at ease in a room full of strangers, especially when they inevitably asked about her music.

Olivia: Of course. What time again?

Sarah: 7. Don't even think about canceling.

By the time the sun began to set, Olivia was already regretting her decision to go. She stood in front of her closet, trying to decide if she cared enough to put in any effort. Finally, she grabbed a black sweater and jeans, deciding they were casual enough to avoid attention but still presentable.

She picked up her coat and violin case, not because she intended to play but because the thought of leaving it behind made her feel strangely uneasy. Slinging the strap over her shoulder, she stepped out into the crisp evening air, her footsteps echoing softly on the quiet street.

By the time Olivia arrived, the party was already in full swing. Warm laughter and the clink of glasses spilled out onto the porch, a stark contrast to the solitude she'd just left behind. She rang the bell, and moments later, Sarah opened the door with an exaggerated gasp, pulling her into a tight hug.

"You're here! And you brought the violin! Are you finally going to play something for us?"

Olivia managed a smile, shaking her head. "No way. I just… didn't want to leave it at home."

Sarah looked at her knowingly but didn't press. Instead, she dragged Olivia into the living room, where a group of people were huddled around the fireplace.

The evening passed in a blur of introductions, small talk, and glasses of wine. Olivia found herself seated on a couch, half-listening to a story about someone's trip to Paris when her thoughts drifted back to the violin in Theo's shop.

Her hands itched to play it, to feel its weight against her shoulder, to draw the bow across its strings. She shook her head, trying to focus on the conversation, but the sensation was so strong it was almost physical.

Later that night, Olivia returned home, her limbs heavy with exhaustion. The forced socializing had drained her, and the wine hadn't helped. She unlocked the door to her small apartment, pushed it open with her shoulder, and dropped her bag by the entrance. The quiet hit her immediately, stark and still compared to the noise of Sarah's party.

She glanced at the clock on the wall, nearly midnight. It was later than she'd planned to stay, but Sarah had been insistent, pulling her into conversation after conversation. A sigh escaped her lips as she flicked on the lights, illuminating the familiar, cozy space.

Her violin case hung awkwardly from her shoulder, and she carefully set it down on the coffee table. It had been her father's, and though it was worn from years of use, she treated it like a priceless relic. The thought made her chest tighten. She rubbed at her temples and wandered into the kitchen.

As she filled a glass of water, her mind replayed the evening's events: strangers asking what she did for work, nodding politely when she mentioned music, and then the inevitable follow-up—"Oh, you should play something for us!" The thought made her stomach clench. She hated the attention, hated how people's expectations made her feel like an impostor.

The sound of her boots scuffing against the floor broke the silence as she moved back to the living room. She reached for the TV remote, eager to distract herself with something mindless.

And that's when she noticed it.

Her violin case was open.

Her initial thought was practical; perhaps she had forgotten to close it. However, the rationality of the thought didn't hold. She never forgot to latch it. Never. Years of habit made sure of that.

A slight chill ran down her spine as she stepped closer. The case lay on the table, its lid angled slightly upward, the interior neatly arranged as always. Her violin rested in its proper spot, snug and secure, and her bow lay parallel to it. But there was something else. Something that hadn't been there before.

A folded piece of paper, stark white against the dark velvet lining.

Her heart stuttered in her chest. Slowly, she reached for the note, her fingers trembling. The paper was smooth, heavy-stock, and when she unfolded it, she froze.

The handwriting was unfamiliar, slanted, and elegant, like something from a different era.

"The music you seek is not your own. Follow the melody."

Her pulse quickened. She turned the paper over, searching for more, an address, a name, anything, but it was blank. She reread the words, the weight of them settling in her stomach.

Her gaze darted around the room, scanning for anything out of place. The air felt different now, heavier, like someone had been there and left just moments before she got home.

She walked to the door and checked the lock; it was secure, just as she had left it. The windows were shut tight, and nothing else seemed out of place. But the feeling lingered, a prickle at the back of her neck, as though she were being watched.

She stepped back into the living room, the silence pressing in on her. Her violin case sat there, innocent and undisturbed, as if daring her to question what she knew was impossible.

Her fingers tightened around the note, crumpling its edges. Her breaths came shallow, her mind racing with questions she didn't know how to answer.

Had someone been here?

Had she forgotten to close the case?

Or worse, had she been so distracted when she got home that she hadn't noticed someone following her?

Her stomach twisted at the thought. She'd felt off all evening—at Sarah's party, on the walk home, even now. But she'd chalked it up to exhaustion. Now, she wasn't so sure.

She glanced back at the violin case, the note's cryptic message echoing in her mind: "Follow the melody."

What melody? What did it mean?

As she stood there, frozen, a sound cut through the silence. It was a single note, low and mournful like the opening of a symphony played on an unseen stage. It vibrated through her chest, sending a shiver down her spine.

Her violin was silent. The sound wasn't coming from anywhere she could see, yet it resonated, filling the room with its eerie presence.

She stumbled back, clutching the edge of the couch for support. The note swelled, and for a moment, she swore she saw something flicker, a shadow in the corner of her vision.

And then, as suddenly as it had begun, the sound stopped.

The silence that followed was so absolute and heavy that it made her ears ring.

Her breaths came in shallow gasps, her fingers still clutching the note as though it might anchor her to reality. She turned, her gaze darting to the violin and the locked door.

She wasn't alone. She was sure of it. But whoever—or whatever—had been there was gone now, leaving her with nothing but questions and the faint echo of a haunting note.

The following day, Olivia found herself standing outside Theo's shop. She hadn't planned to go, but something had drawn her there, like a magnet she couldn't resist.

The bell above the door jingled as she stepped inside. Theo looked up from the counter, his expression unreadable.

"You're back," he said.

Olivia nodded, her fingers clutching the strap of her bag. "I need to see the violin again."

Theo studied her for a long moment before gesturing toward the stand where the violin rested. "Go ahead."

This time, Olivia didn't hesitate. She reached out and picked it up; its weight was solid and familiar. As she raised it to her shoulder, Theo stepped closer, watching her intently.

"Play," he said.

Her fingers found the strings, her bow poised, and then she drew it across the strings. The sound that emerged was low and haunting, vibrating through her like a pulse. She closed her eyes, and the melody began to take shape, a song she had never heard before but somehow knew.

Images flashed behind her closed lids: a cliffside bathed in mist, a cottage with a red door, a man's silhouette against the setting sun.

She opened her eyes, her breath coming in short gasps. Theo was staring at her, his expression a mix of shock and understanding.

"What did you see?" he asked.

Olivia shook her head, her hands trembling. "I don't know," she whispered. "But I think… I think it's trying to tell me something."

Theo's question hung in the air like the last lingering note of a symphony.

"What did you see?"

Olivia's hands trembled as she lowered the violin, her breath uneven. The vivid and real images that flashed in her mind were unlike anything she had ever experienced. She felt as though she had been transported to another world, one layered with fragments of memory and meaning just out of reach.

"I… I'm not sure," she said finally, her voice barely above a whisper. "A place—a cliff, a red cottage. And a man, but I couldn't see his face."

Theo nodded slowly, his gray eyes sharp with understanding—or something close to it. "It's showing you something," he said. "Something it wants you to find."

Olivia frowned, gripping the violin tighter. "It?"

"The violin," Theo said simply, gesturing to the instrument still clutched in her hands. "You're connected to it now. It's not just showing you a place; it's leading you to it."

The weight of his words settled over her, thick and oppressive. She wanted to argue, to insist it was just a trick of her imagination, but she couldn't. The pull she had felt, the haunting note, the images all fit together in a way she didn't understand but couldn't deny.

Theo stepped closer, his voice low. "I've seen this before, Olivia. The visions. The connection. The questions. Once you start, you can't ignore it."

"Then what do I do?" she asked, the desperation in her voice surprising even her.

"You keep playing," Theo said, his tone steady. "You follow the melody, just like the note said. It will lead you where you need to go."

Olivia looked down at the violin, its dark wood gleaming under the shop's warm lights. For the first time, it felt like more than an instrument; it felt like a question she had no choice but to answer.

Chapter 3
FUGUE

T he melody still rang in Olivia's ears when she left the shop. She stepped into the crisp morning air, the sound of the door's bell fading behind her. The streets of London were already alive with people, the steady hum of cars and distant chatter filling the space around her. But Olivia barely noticed.

Her fingers ached from gripping the violin, and her mind spun with questions. Although she had tucked it back into its case, she could still feel its heavy and constant weight against her shoulder.

The images she had seen while playing swirled in her mind like fragments of a dream, a cliff shrouded in mist, a red cottage, a man standing in the distance. She had never been to such a place, but something about it felt familiar, as though it had been waiting for her all along.

Her steps slowed as she reached the corner of her street, the pull of the violin urging her to turn back. She shook her head, forcing herself to keep walking. She wasn't ready to face whatever answers it held, not yet.

When Olivia entered her apartment, she carefully set the violin case down, almost afraid to open it. She wandered into the kitchen, pouring herself a cup of coffee and wrapping her hands around the warm mug. She stared at the counter, her thoughts racing.

Could Theo be correct? Could the violin be guiding her somewhere? The logical part of her mind resisted the idea, but her gut, her instincts, whatever piece of her had inherited her father's connection to music, believed it.

Her gaze drifted to the violin case on the table. It sat there, still and silent, but its presence was undeniable. It was as though it were waiting for her to pick it up again, to play the melody and let it guide her further into whatever mystery it held.

She closed her eyes and exhaled slowly, her fingers drumming against the side of her mug. "This is crazy," she muttered to herself.

But the pull was too strong to ignore.

Later that evening, Olivia sat on the edge of her bed, the violin cradled in her lap. The apartment was dim, the only light coming from a small lamp on the nightstand. Her hands shook as she tightened the bow, the movement mechanical and familiar.

She placed the violin against her shoulder, her breath catching as her fingers found the strings. Its weight felt heavier now, as though it carried not just music... but history.

She drew the bow across the strings, the sound low and resonant, and the melody emerged again, haunting and otherworldly. It wrapped around her, pulling her into its depths.

Her vision blurred as the world around her shifted. The walls of her apartment dissolved, replaced by an endless expanse of gray mist. She was no longer sitting; she was standing on the edge of a cliff, the wind whipping her hair as the sound of waves crashed far below.

Ahead of her was the red cottage, its door slightly ajar. The man stood in front of it, his back to her. He was tall, his shoulders broad, but his features were obscured by shadow.

Olivia took a step forward, her heart pounding. "Who are you?" she called, her voice thin against the roar of the wind.

The man turned slightly, his face still hidden. But the melody swelled before she could get closer, pulling her back.

She gasped as her apartment came rushing back into view, her bow slipping from her fingers. She clutched the violin tightly, her chest heaving.

The vision had felt so real, so tangible like she could reach out and touch it.

And in her mind, the haunting melody continued to play.

Chapter 4

THEO CALLAHAN

The next time Olivia entered Callahan Antiques, it was raining. Fat droplets drummed against the shop's awning, spilling over its edges in tiny cascades. She shook off her umbrella just inside the door, the bell jingling faintly overhead. The rich scent of aged wood and polish welcomed her, grounding her.

Theo stood at the counter, hunched over a small collection of tools spread across its polished surface. His hands moved with a surgeon's precision, carefully adjusting the bridge of an antique violin. The soft creak of the floorboards beneath her feet drew his attention, and when he looked up, his gray eyes flickered with surprise.

"You're back," he said, setting the violin down gently. His brow lifted ever so slightly, and a faint smile played at the corner of his lips, though it didn't reach his eyes.

Olivia shifted her weight, clutching the strap of her bag. "I can't seem to stay away," she admitted, her tone lighter than she felt.

Theo straightened, wiping his hands on a cloth before tossing it onto the counter. "Well, you've certainly taken an interest in my most enigmatic piece." He nodded toward the violin resting on its stand nearby. "Not that I blame you. It has that effect on people."

Her eyes were drawn to the instrument, just as they had been the first time she saw it. It seemed alive even from across the room, its polished surface catching the muted light filtering through the rain-speckled windows. She stepped closer, her pulse quickening as the familiar pull tightened around her.

"What's its story?" she asked, her voice barely above a whisper.

Theo's expression shifted, his usual guarded demeanor softening into something more thoughtful. "You really want to know?"

Olivia nodded.

He gestured toward a pair of armchairs tucked into the far corner of the shop. "Let's sit. It's not a short story."

The antique shop seemed to hold its breath as they crossed the room, their footsteps muffled by an intricately patterned rug. The shelves were packed with relics from forgotten eras, timeworn books with cracked spines, brass candlesticks that glinted dully in the dim light, and instruments that seemed to hum faintly with dormant music. A grandfather clock ticked steadily near the back wall, its rhythmic chime adding a quiet sense of gravity to the space.

As Olivia settled into the chair, it let out a faint creak. Outside, the rain continued its steady drumming, punctuating the silence as Theo took the seat opposite her.

Theo leaned forward, resting his elbows on his knees and clasping his hands together. He stared at the floor momentarily as though searching for the right place to begin.

"The violin came to me about seven years ago," he said finally, his voice low and even. "I was living in Vienna at the time, working as a restorer for a small shop in the city center. The owner, Klaus, was… one of a kind. He had this uncanny ability to breathe life back into instruments that most people would've written off as beyond repair. It was like he could see the soul of the music trapped inside them."

A faint smile tugged at Theo's lips, though it quickly faded. "One day, a man came in with a violin. It was in terrible shape—warped wood, peeling varnish, cracks in the soundboard. He said it had been in his family for generations but had always been… different."

Olivia tilted her head. "Different, how?"

Theo's brow furrowed as his fingers tapped restlessly against the armrest. "He wouldn't say. But he looked desperate. He kept clutching the violin like it was the only thing keeping him grounded, and he said it needed to be restored—no matter the cost."

"And Klaus agreed?"

Theo nodded. "We both did. It was a challenge, sure, but we'd never turned anyone away before. We started working on it the next day, and… that's when things got strange."

"Strange how?" Olivia pressed, leaning forward slightly.

Theo's gaze shifted toward the violin on its stand, his expression darkening. "The wood… it didn't behave like normal wood. It was harder, denser. Every time we tried to make adjustments, it resisted us—almost like it didn't want to be touched. And the sound… even unfinished, it was unlike anything I'd ever heard. It wasn't just beautiful. It was… eerie. Ethereal."

He paused, his fingers tightening around the edge of the chair. "The man came back for it months later. But when I saw him, I almost didn't recognize him."

"What do you mean?" Olivia asked, her stomach twisting.

"He looked… drained," Theo said, his voice dropping to a near-whisper. "Like he'd aged ten years in half that time. His hands shook when he held the violin, and his eyes… were haunted. He said he needed to leave Vienna immediately but wouldn't tell us why."

"And did you ever see him again?"

"No," Theo admitted. "But about a year later, I heard that he'd disappeared. Just… vanished without a trace."

Theo's eyes flickered back to Olivia, his expression unreadable. "The violin turned up here a few years later, shipped anonymously in a plain wooden crate. No note, no return address. At first, I thought it was a coincidence. But now…" He trailed off, shaking his head.

"Now you think it's more than that," Olivia finished for him.

Theo nodded slowly. "Every time I've tried to sell it, something's gone wrong. Buyers back out, shipments get lost... it always finds its way back here. And the people who play it..." He hesitated, his jaw tightening. "They all say the same thing: it feels alive."

A chill ran down Olivia's spine, her skin prickling like the violin was watching her from its stand.

"Why keep it?" she asked, her voice barely above a whisper.

"Because I'm afraid of what will happen if I don't," Theo said simply. "This violin... it's not just an instrument. It's a doorway. And destroying it won't close that door; it'll only make things worse."

Olivia leaned back in her chair, the weight of Theo's words pressing down on her. She wanted to believe it was all some elaborate story, a superstition born from coincidence and fear. But the pull she felt toward the violin was undeniable.

"And you?" she asked quietly. "Have you ever played it?"

Theo's expression darkened. He looked away, his hands gripping the edges of the armrest tightly. "Once," he admitted, his voice strained.

"What happened?"

"It showed me things," Theo said, his words slow and deliberate. "Memories I'd tried to forget. Things I didn't want to face. And after that... it was like a piece of me had been taken. For weeks, I couldn't sleep. I couldn't think. Every time I closed my eyes, I heard that melody, over and over."

Olivia's chest tightened, her heart pounding in her ears. "Then why keep it here? Why not get rid of it?"

Theo's gaze snapped back to hers, his gray eyes hard. "Because it's not done yet," he said. "It's waiting for something or someone. And now, for whatever reason, it's chosen you."

Theo stood abruptly, crossing the room to retrieve the violin. He held it out to Olivia, his expression grim. "Here," he said. "Play it again."

Her hands trembled as she took the instrument, its weight familiar but no less intimidating. She raised it to her shoulder, her fingers brushing against the strings.

The first note was soft, almost hesitant, but the melody began to take shape as she played. It was the same haunting tune as before, but now it felt sharper, more deliberate, as though the violin were guiding her.

Images flooded her mind: the cliffside bathed in mist, the red cottage, the silhouette of a man standing in the distance. But there were new details, sunlight glinting off the water, the sound of waves crashing, the faint scent of salt in the air.

Her breathing quickened as the vision deepened, the world around her fading until she was standing on that cliff, the wind whipping through her hair.

And then, just as suddenly, it was gone.

Olivia lowered the violin, her hands shaking. "It's leading me somewhere," she said breathlessly.

Theo nodded, his expression somber. "Then you have to follow it."

Chapter 5

THE HIDDEN COMPARTMENT

The walk home from Callahan Antiques felt heavier than usual, each step laden with the weight of Theo's words.

"It's waiting for something or someone. And now, for whatever reason, it's chosen you."

The violin case in her hand felt almost alive, its weight pressing into her palm as if it resisted being carried. Theo had insisted she take it with her, his expression grim but resolute. "If it's speaking to you," he had said, "then you need to listen."

The streets were eerily quiet, the soft mist in the air dulling the sounds of the city. When she reached her apartment, Olivia placed the case carefully on the dining table, her fingers brushing against its latches.

Her eyes lingered on the instrument as she shrugged off her coat. This wasn't just any violin; she knew that now. It was the same one that had pulled her into visions of cliffs and cottages and brought her here in search of answers.

But even as she opened the case and stared at its polished surface, she couldn't shake the sense that she was walking deeper into something she didn't understand.

This wasn't just a violin.

This was the beginning of something much bigger.

The next morning, Olivia woke with the melody still playing in her mind, a haunting refrain woven into the edges of her consciousness. Her dreams had been fragmented—visions of mist-shrouded cliffs and the faint echo of waves crashing against unseen rocks. She had tossed and turned for hours, but the violin's pull lingered, refusing to release its grip.

Her apartment was unnervingly quiet, as though the very walls were waiting. Morning sunlight filtered through the sheer curtains, casting long shadows across the floor. The violin sat on the dining table in its open case, its polished wood catching the light.

She hadn't meant to bring it home from Theo's shop. But as the evening wore on, leaving it behind had felt impossible, like trying to walk away from a part of herself. Now, as she stared at the instrument, her chest tightened with awe and trepidation.

Olivia moved closer, her fingers tracing the edge of the violin's body. Its surface was smooth and flawless, except for the faint carvings she had noticed before—ornate patterns that were too intricate to be purely decorative. As her thumb passed over the underside of the instrument, she froze.

There was a line.

At first, she thought it was a scratch, but as she tilted the violin under the light, she saw it was too straight, too deliberate. Her pulse quickened, a sudden tightness spreading through her chest. She leaned closer, holding her breath as her fingers probed the faint seam.

The violin was cool to the touch, the wood almost unnaturally smooth. She pressed her fingernail against the line, testing its resistance. Nothing moved.

Olivia's brow furrowed as she pressed harder, her heart pounding now, each beat echoing in her ears. Then, with a soft click, the seam gave way.

Her breath caught as a hidden compartment slid open, revealing a tightly folded piece of parchment nestled within.

For a moment, Olivia didn't move. Her fingers hovered over the parchment, her breath shallow and unsteady. The air seemed heavier now, charged with something she couldn't name. Slowly, she reached inside, her fingertips brushing against the brittle edges of the paper.

It smelled faintly of age, an earthy, almost musty scent that sent a shiver down her spine. As she carefully unfolded it, the parchment revealed a series of notes and symbols scrawled in dark, uneven ink.

At first glance, it appeared to be sheet music, but something about it was… wrong. The notes were arranged in a pattern she didn't recognize, interspersed with strange markings that looked like ancient runes. The melody itself was incomplete, trailing off abruptly at the bottom of the page, as though whoever had written it had been interrupted.

Her hands trembled as she stared at the parchment, her mind racing with questions. What was this? Who had hidden it here?

And why did it feel like it was meant for her?

The sudden buzz of her phone shattered the silence, making Olivia jump. Her hand jerked, almost tearing the fragile parchment. She snatched the phone from the table, her breath still uneven.

"Hello?"

"You've been quiet," Theo's voice came through the line, steady but laced with curiosity. "How's it going with the violin?"

Olivia hesitated, her eyes darting back to the parchment spread out in front of her. "I… I found something," she said finally, her voice tinged with disbelief.

There was a pause. "What do you mean, you found something?"

"I think… I think the violin has a hidden compartment," Olivia said, the words tumbling out in a rush. "There was something inside—a piece of parchment. It looks like sheet music, but it's… different."

Theo's response was immediate. "I'm on my way."

Twenty minutes later, Theo arrived, his dark coat damp from the persistent mist outside. His eyes darted around the room, lingering on the violin and the parchment spread across the table.

Without a word, he shrugged off his coat and approached the table, his movements deliberate. His gaze was sharp, intense, as he leaned over the parchment.

"Let me see," he said, his voice low.

Olivia handed it to him, watching as his fingers lightly traced the edges of the brittle paper. His brow furrowed, and his lips pressed into a thin line as he studied the strange symbols.

"This is… different," he murmured, his voice barely audible.

"What do you mean?" Olivia asked, inching closer.

Theo tapped one of the markings. "These aren't just musical notes. They're symbols—alchemical, maybe. There was a time when people believed music could transcend the physical world, that certain combinations of tones and frequencies could influence the soul—or open doors to something else entirely."

Olivia's stomach tightened. "And you think that's what this is?"

"I don't know," Theo admitted, his fingers brushing over the parchment. "But whoever created this wasn't just composing music. They were trying to… communicate something."

They worked in silence for hours, Theo jotting notes in a small leather-bound journal while Olivia tried to decipher the incomplete melody. The symbols seemed to shift under the light, their meaning always just out of reach.

Finally, Theo leaned back in his chair, exhaling sharply. "We're not going to solve this by staring at it. Play it."

Olivia froze, her hands clenching into fists. "What if it's dangerous?"

Theo's gaze was steady. "It's already dangerous. But if we don't try to understand it, we'll never know what we're dealing with."

She hesitated, her chest tightening with a mix of fear and anticipation. Finally, she stood, lifting the violin from its case. The instrument felt heavier than usual, its surface cool against her skin.

Taking a deep breath, Olivia placed the bow against the strings. The first note was soft, tentative, but as she continued, the melody began to take shape. It was haunting, otherworldly, each note resonating deep within her.

As the final note rang out, the room seemed to shift. The air grew heavy, and a faint hum vibrated through the floor.

The world blurred, the edges of the room dissolving into a haze of light and shadow. Olivia felt herself being pulled forward, her surroundings fading until she was standing on the edge of the cliff from her visions.

The wind was stronger this time, whipping her hair around her face. The ocean stretched out before her, vast and endless, its waves crashing violently against the rocks below.

In the distance, the red cottage stood, its door slightly ajar.

Olivia moved toward it, her footsteps crunching against the rocky ground. Her breath came in shallow gasps as she reached the door, her fingers trembling as she pushed it open.

Inside, the air was thick with the scent of salt and something metallic. A table sat in the center of the room, and on it lay another piece of parchment, identical to the one she had found in the violin.

A figure stood in the shadows, his back to her.

"Who are you?" Olivia demanded, her voice breaking.

The figure turned slowly, but before she could see his face, the vision dissolved.

Olivia gasped as she was pulled back into the present, the violin slipping from her hands and clattering to the floor. Her knees buckled, and she gripped the edge of the table, struggling to steady herself.

Theo was at her side in an instant, his hands on her shoulders. "What happened?"

"I saw it again," Olivia whispered, her voice shaking. "The cliff. The cottage. There was… another piece of music."

Theo's expression darkened. "Then this isn't over," he said quietly. "Not by a long shot."

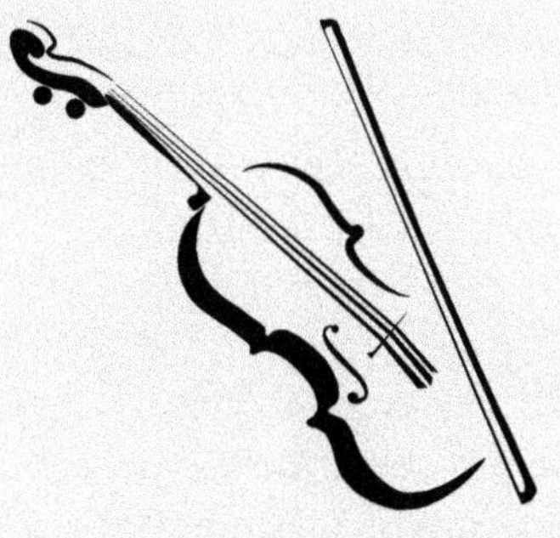

Chapter 6

A MOTHER'S SECRET

The hours after Theo left were restless. Olivia sat in her apartment long into the night, staring at the violin case as the fragments of her vision swirled in her mind. The image of the red cottage loomed larger than before, a beacon pulling her toward a truth she wasn't sure she was ready to face.

But the memory of her mother's guarded expressions, her careful avoidance of questions about Olivia's father, now struck her with undeniable clarity. Evelyn Hart had always been a master at sidestepping the past, deflecting curiosity with gentle reassurances.

Not this time.

By morning, Olivia's resolve was unshakable. If the violin held the key to her father's disappearance, then Evelyn had answers. And Olivia was determined to get them.

The frost-coated grass crunched under Olivia's boots as she stepped onto her mother's porch, the violin case clutched tightly in her hand. The strap dug into her palm, the familiar weight of the instrument grounding her even as her thoughts spiraled.

She stared at the front door, her stomach knotting. Her breaths came shallow and quick, each visible in the cold morning air. The house loomed before her, its weathered shutters and neatly trimmed garden unchanged since her childhood. For years, this had been her safe haven. Now, it felt like stepping into enemy territory.

Summoning her courage, Olivia knocked. The sound was too loud, too sharp, breaking the stillness of the crisp morning.

A moment later, the door opened. Evelyn Hart stood in the doorway, her gray eyes widening slightly at the sight of her daughter.

"Liv," she said, her voice warm but tinged with surprise. Her gaze drifted to the violin case, and something flickered across her face, recognition or perhaps fear. "What brings you here so early?"

Olivia stepped inside without answering, the familiar scent of lavender and old wood washing over her. "I need to talk to you," she said, her tone firmer than expected.

Evelyn hesitated her hand still on the doorknob. "About what?"

Olivia placed the violin case on the coffee table and turned to face her mother. "About Dad. And this."

Evelyn's eyes locked onto the violin case, her posture stiffening. For a moment, she said nothing, her fingers tightening around the edge of the doorframe.

"Let's sit," she said finally, her voice barely audible.

The living room hadn't changed since Olivia's childhood. The faded floral couch sagged slightly in the middle, its cushions softened by years of use. A quilt draped across the armrest, its bright patches starkly contrasting the room's muted tones. The mantle above the fireplace was crowded with porcelain figurines, family photos, and a single unlit candle.

Dust motes danced in the golden shafts of sunlight that streamed through the lace curtains, giving the room an almost ethereal quality. But the warmth of the space couldn't dispel the tension that hung in the air.

Evelyn perched on the edge of her armchair, her back straight and rigid. Olivia sat across from her, leaning forward, her elbows resting on her knees. The violin case between them felt like a barrier, a line drawn in the sand.

"Where do I start?" Olivia said, her voice tight. "The visions? The hidden compartment? Or the fact that this violin seems to pull me into something I don't understand?"

Evelyn flinched, her hands gripping the edge of her chair. "What are you talking about?" she asked, her voice wavering.

"You know exactly what I'm talking about," Olivia shot back, her voice rising. "You've always known. About Dad. About this violin. And you've been keeping it from me."

Evelyn's gaze dropped to her lap, her fingers twisting nervously. "Olivia, please..."

"Don't," Olivia interrupted, her anger spilling over. "Don't tell me to let it go. I can't. Not anymore."

The room fell silent, the faint ticking of the grandfather clock the only sound. Finally, Evelyn looked up, her eyes glistening with unshed tears.

"Your father loved you," she said quietly. "Everything he did, he did to protect you."

Evelyn's voice trembled as she began to speak. Her words were slow and measured, as though each one carried a great weight.

"Your father wasn't just a musician, Liv," she said, her gaze distant. "He was... something else. A seeker, I suppose. He believed that music wasn't just sound, it was a way to connect with the world, history,... things most people couldn't see."

Olivia leaned forward, her breath catching. "What kind of things?"

Evelyn hesitated, her hands wringing in her lap. "Have you ever heard of the 'Lost Harmonies'?"

Olivia shook her head.

"It's a legend," Evelyn continued. "A belief that certain melodies can bridge the gap between worlds. Some people think it's just folklore, but there are others... collectors, scholars, musicians... who believe it's real. Your father was one of them."

"Was that why he disappeared?" Olivia asked, her voice trembling.

Evelyn's shoulders sagged, her gaze dropping to the floor. "He found something, Liv. A violin that had been hidden away for centuries. The people who hired him to retrieve it said it was cursed, but your father didn't believe in curses. He thought it was a key that could unlock the Lost Harmonies."

"And?" Olivia pressed, her stomach twisting.

"And it changed him," Evelyn whispered. "He started having visions, just like you. He'd wake up in the middle of the night, talking about places he'd never been and people he'd never met. He became obsessed with the violin, convinced it was leading him toward something."

Olivia's hands clenched into fists. "And then he vanished."

Evelyn nodded, tears spilling down her cheeks. "I begged him not to go. I told him we didn't need the money and could find another way. But he wouldn't listen. He said he had to finish what he started. And then he… he was gone."

Evelyn's voice broke, and she buried her face in her hands. "I thought it would go away if I didn't talk about it. I thought I could protect you from it. But now…" She looked up, her expression desperate. "Now it's found you."

Olivia's chest ached with a mix of anger and sorrow. "Why didn't you tell me? Why did you let me grow up thinking he abandoned us?"

"I was trying to protect you!" Evelyn cried, her voice cracking. "You were just a child, Liv. How could I tell you that your father disappeared chasing a legend? How could I tell you that he might never come back?"

Olivia stood abruptly, pacing the room. Her fingers brushed against the edge of the violin case as she walked, the cool surface grounding her thoughts.

"This violin is showing me things," she said, her voice steady. "Visions of cliffs, a red cottage, and someone waiting for me. It's connected to Dad; I know it is. And I'm going to find out the truth."

Evelyn's breath hitched. "Please, Liv. Don't go down this path. Whatever your father was searching for, it cost him everything. Don't let it take you too."

Olivia turned to face her mother, her expression resolute. "It's too late for that. I need to know what happened to him. I need to know why this violin chose me."

Chapter 7

CLUES

Olivia stared out her apartment window, her reflection barely visible in the rain-slick glass. The gray sky outside mirrored the heavy storm brewing in her mind. Her mother's words played on an endless loop, each revelation peeling back another layer of the truth she had been shielded from for so long.

Her father hadn't just disappeared, he had been searching for something. Something tied to the violin now sitting on her dining table.

The air in the apartment felt stifling, heavy with unspoken questions. Olivia turned to the violin case, its latches glinting faintly in the dim light. The melody it had played, the haunting otherworldly tune, still hummed at the edges of her consciousness.

Evelyn's warning was clear: Don't go down this path. Don't let it consume you.

But it was too late. The path had already found her.

As she crossed the room, her eyes fell on the tattered leather journal she had taken from her mother's bookshelf before leaving. It had been tucked away, hidden among old photo albums and unopened letters, but something about it had caught her attention. The initials on the cover, J.H., were unmistakable. It belonged to her father.

Olivia sank onto the couch, the journal balanced on her knees. The leather was soft, worn from years of use, and the faint scent of old paper rose as she carefully opened it. Her father's neat handwriting filled the first few pages, and his notes were detailed and methodical.

She traced her fingers over the words, her throat tightening. This was a piece of him, a fragment of the man she had spent her life searching for.

The journal began innocuously enough: lists of concerts, notes on compositions, and sketches of melodies. But as Olivia flipped through the pages, the tone began to shift. The handwriting grew messier, the sentences shorter and fragmented, as though written in haste.

"The monastery holds more than relics. The monks know something they won't say. I can feel it in the air…like the walls are breathing."

A chill ran down Olivia's spine. She turned the page.

"The violin is unlike any I've encountered. Its sound is… alive. It speaks to me, though I can't explain how. I played it today, and it was as if the room disappeared for a moment. I was somewhere else entirely. A cliff. The sea. A red door."

Olivia's breath hitched. She scanned the entry again, her heart pounding. He had seen it too. The same vision.

The air in the apartment seemed to grow colder as Olivia continued reading. Her father's entries became more erratic, and the language disjointed.

"The collectors won't stop. They want the violin for themselves. They don't understand what it can do, what it's capable of. If it falls into the wrong hands…"

The words trailed off, replaced by a jagged line of ink that cut across the page. Olivia's fingers tightened around the journal.

The next entry was dated just days before his disappearance.

"The melody is incomplete. I found the first piece, but the rest eludes me. The answers lie with the others. I must find them before it's too late."

"The others?" Olivia whispered, her voice barely audible.

She turned the page, but it was blank.

The room was silent except for the faint ticking of the clock on the wall. Olivia leaned back against the couch, her mind racing. Her father had been searching for something: other pieces of the melody hidden in places like those she had seen in her visions.

She closed the journal, the leather warm beneath her palms. Her thoughts flickered back to the vision of the red cottage and the skeletal figure pointing toward the table. There had been something there a second piece of parchment.

Her phone buzzed on the coffee table, breaking her concentration. She grabbed it, her breath catching when she saw Theo's name.

"You've been busy," Theo said when she answered, his tone laced with curiosity.

"I found something," Olivia said, her voice tight. "My father's journal. He wrote about the violin and the visions."

There was a pause. "What else did he say?"

"He mentioned others," Olivia said, her gaze drifting back to the journal. "Pieces of the melody. He was looking for them."

Theo exhaled sharply. "Then he was closer than I thought."

"Closer to what?" Olivia asked.

"To whatever the violin is leading you toward," Theo said. "If your father was searching for the melody, it means he believed it could be completed. And if that's true…"

"Then it's not over," Olivia finished her voice barely above a whisper.

The next morning, Olivia sat in Theo's shop, the journal open on the counter between them. The air was thick with the scent of aged wood and varnish, and the faint strains of classical music played softly from the radio.

Theo leaned over the journal, his brow furrowed in concentration. "This part about the collectors," he said, tapping the page. "Do you know who they are?"

Olivia shook her head. "My mother didn't mention them. But she said they were the ones who hired my father to retrieve the violin."

Theo nodded slowly, his expression thoughtful. "That would explain the lengths they went to. If they knew what the violin was capable of…"

He trailed off, his gaze shifting to the instrument resting on its stand nearby.

"What about the melody?" Olivia asked, her voice breaking the silence.

Theo straightened, his gray eyes sharp. "If your father was right, and there are other pieces, we need to find them. But first, we have to figure out where to start."

Olivia pulled the journal closer, flipping back to the entry about the monastery. "He mentioned a monastery in the Swiss Alps. That's where he found the violin."

Theo nodded, his expression grim. "Then that's where we go."

The decision felt monumental, like crossing an invisible threshold. Olivia glanced at the violin, its dark wood gleaming in the dim light. The thought of leaving everything behind— her apartment, her job, and her carefully constructed life—was daunting. But the pull of the violin was stronger, undeniable.

"You're sure about this?" Theo asked, his tone measured.

"I don't have a choice," Olivia said, her voice steady. "If my father was willing to risk everything for this, then I have to see it through."

Theo studied her for a moment before nodding. "Then we'll leave tomorrow."

That night, Olivia stood in the dim glow of her bedroom lamp, staring at the open suitcase on her bed. She hesitated with every item she placed inside: a sweater her mother had knitted, worn jeans, sturdy boots. Each choice felt loaded with meaning, as though the contents of this small bag would somehow dictate the outcome of her journey.

Her hands shook as she folded her favorite scarf and tucked it into the corner of the case. What did one pack for an expedition into the unknown? She didn't know how long she'd be gone or even what she'd find when she arrived, but the thought of leaving unprepared gnawed at her.

The journal sat on her bedside table, its worn leather cover catching the light. She reached for it, running her fingers over the embossed initials: J.H. Her father's handwriting—his thoughts, fears, and discoveries—felt like a lifeline now. She tucked the journal carefully into the bag, placing it next to a small travel notebook and a pen.

Her eyes drifted to the violin case resting against the wall. The sight of it sent a wave of emotion crashing over her—a mix of fear, hope, and a deep yearning she couldn't name. She crossed the room and knelt beside it, her hands tracing the smooth edges.

The violin felt heavier now, as though it held her father's secrets and the weight of everything left unspoken between them. Her chest tightened, and for a moment, she couldn't breathe.

"What am I doing?" she whispered, her voice breaking in the stillness.

She closed her eyes, gripping the case tightly as a tear slid down her cheek. Her mother's warnings echoed in her mind, but so did her father's notes, his urgent scrawl insisting that the melody was incomplete.

Finally, she rose and placed the violin case gently beside her bag.

When she climbed into bed, the apartment felt quieter than ever, the silence pressing against her like a second skin. Her thoughts refused to settle, spinning with fragments of her father's journal and the haunting vision of the red cottage.

The melody returned, faint and insistent, weaving through her consciousness like a thread pulling her forward. It was both a comfort and a curse, a reminder that this journey was no longer a choice but a calling.

As the hours ticked by and the city outside faded into stillness, Olivia stared at the ceiling, her heart pounding with equal parts fear and determination.

Tomorrow, she would leave behind everything she had ever known and begin her search for the truth. There would be no turning back.

Chapter 8

THE IRISH VILLAGE

The morning began in a flurry of movement and nervous energy. Olivia barely remembered stepping into the shower or pulling on her clothes, her mind already racing with the weight of what lay ahead. The packed bag and violin case sat by the door like silent witnesses to her decision.

Theo arrived just after dawn, his car idling on the curb. He leaned against the hood, his sharp eyes scanning the quiet street as Olivia locked her apartment for what felt like the last time.

"Ready?" he asked when she joined him, his tone calm but edged with something unreadable.

"Not really," Olivia admitted, gripping the violin case tightly. "But I don't think I ever will be."

Theo offered a reassuring nod before loading her bag into the trunk. "Let's get moving. The airport's a bit of a drive."

The trip to the airport passed in a blur. Olivia stared out the window, her fingers drumming against the violin case on her lap. The city slipped away behind them, replaced by rolling fields and the occasional cluster of houses. The early morning light cast long shadows over the landscape, giving everything a dreamlike quality.

"You okay?" Theo asked, glancing at her.

"Yeah," she said, though her voice lacked conviction.

She leaned her head against the window, the cool glass soothing against her temple. Her thoughts spiraled, her mother's warnings, her father's journal, the haunting melody that seemed to play on a loop in her mind. It was like the violin was alive, whispering secrets she couldn't yet understand.

Before she realized it, her eyelids grew heavy, and she slipped into a restless sleep.

She was standing on the edge of the cliff again.

The wind tore at her hair and clothes, the salt spray stinging her cheeks. Below, the waves roared as they crashed against the jagged rocks. She turned, her gaze drawn to the red cottage in the distance.

This time, it was closer. She could see the chipped paint on the door and the weeds growing in wild tangles around the foundation. The skeletal figure was there too, its form cloaked in shadow. It raised a hand, pointing toward the cottage, and Olivia felt her feet move forward as though pulled by an invisible force.

The melody swelled, rich and haunting, weaving through the air like a siren's call. Each note vibrated through her chest, filling her with dread and longing.

As she reached the door, her hand trembled. She pushed it open slowly, the hinges groaning in protest. The interior was dim, but her eyes immediately fell on the table in the center of the room. A piece of parchment lay there, illuminated by a shaft of golden light.

When she stepped forward to grab it, the room shifted. The walls dissolved into mist, the floor disappearing beneath her feet. She fell into darkness, the melody fading into a hollow echo.

"Olivia. Olivia!"

Her eyes snapped open to find Theo shaking her shoulder gently, his brow furrowed with concern.

"We're here," he said, his voice steady.

Olivia sat up, her heart pounding as the vision lingered in the edges of her mind. She glanced out the window, blinking at the airport looming ahead.

"Sorry," she murmured, brushing a hand through her hair. "I must've dozed off."

"You were talking in your sleep," Theo said, his tone careful. "Something about a cottage and… music?"

Olivia's stomach twisted. "It was just a dream," she said quickly, though they both knew it was more than that.

Theo didn't press the issue. Instead, he pulled into the parking lot and turned off the engine. "Let's go," he said, grabbing her bag from the back seat.

The airport was bustling, filled with the clatter of luggage wheels and the hum of announcements over the intercom. Olivia moved through the crowd in a daze, her grip on the violin case so tight her knuckles turned white.

The steady rhythm of the airport, people lining up at security, and the muffled roar of jet engines faded into the background. Every step felt like crossing an invisible threshold, further distancing her from the safety of home and deeper into the unknown.

She barely registered the flight itself, just a blur of check-ins, the low hum of conversation on the plane, and the steady roar of the engines as they carried her over the Atlantic. Theo sat beside her, flipping through a notebook filled with annotated maps and cryptic notes. His focused energy grounded her, even as her own thoughts spiraled.

The faint melody hummed in her mind, growing louder as the hours passed, like a soft but unrelenting tug at her consciousness. When the plane touched down, Olivia felt like she had been running a mental marathon.

The overcast sky and cool breeze in Ireland greeted them like old friends. Olivia stepped off the plane, her boots crunching against the pavement, and felt a strange sense of anticipation settle over her.

The drive from the airport to the monastery wound through narrow country roads, the landscape shifting from quaint villages to sprawling fields bordered by low stone walls. The scent of damp earth and peat fires mingled with the crisp air, creating a soothing and strangely alive atmosphere.

Theo remained quiet as he navigated the winding roads, his focus split between the map on his lap and the road ahead. Olivia sat back, her gaze drifting over the landscape as her thoughts lingered on the vision.

The monastery came into view as they rounded a bend—a sprawling stone structure perched on a hill, its spires reaching toward the clouds. It was imposing, its gray stone walls weathered by centuries of wind and rain.

Olivia felt the melody stir again, stronger now, resonating through her chest like a heartbeat.

The air grew colder as they climbed the hill toward the monastery. As she stepped through the arched entrance, the faint scent of moss and stone filled Olivia's lungs. Inside, the silence was profound, broken only by the soft echoes of their footsteps on the flagstone floor.

A monk greeted them, his expression calm but curious. Theo explained their interest in the monastery's history, carefully omitting the more supernatural elements of their quest.

The monk led them to the library, a vast room filled with towering shelves and the faint scent of parchment and aged wood. Olivia's fingers brushed against the spines of the books as they walked, her heart racing with anticipation.

"This is where your father was," Theo murmured, his voice low.

Olivia turned to him, her chest tightening. "Then maybe we'll find what he was looking for."

They spent hours combing through the library's archives, the weight of history pressing down on them with every page turn.

Theo worked methodically, scanning old maps and journals, while Olivia focused on the music manuscripts.

It was late afternoon when Olivia found a fragment of parchment tucked between the pages of an ancient tome. Her breath caught as she unfolded it, the symbols and notes instantly familiar.

"The second piece," she whispered, her hands trembling.

Theo looked over her shoulder, his eyes narrowing. "It's incomplete, just like the first one."

"But it's something," Olivia said, clutching the parchment tightly.

As she held it, a sudden warmth spread through her fingers, and the world seemed to shift. The melody surged in her mind, louder and more urgent, pulling her back to the cliffside.

The red cottage appeared again, clearer this time, and she could see the faint outline of a figure standing at the window. The vision faded just as quickly, leaving her breathless and unsteady.

They left the monastery as the sun dipped below the horizon, the parchment carefully folded in Olivia's bag. The air was colder now, and the weight of their discovery pressed heavily on her shoulders.

"The pieces are out there," Theo said as they drove back to their lodging. "We just have to find them."

Olivia nodded, her determination hardening. The melody was leading her somewhere, and she wouldn't stop until she found it.

This was only the beginning.

Chapter 9

THE LEGEND OF THE VIOLIN

The road to the hostel was narrow and winding, bordered by rows of tall, spindly trees that shivered in the evening breeze. Theo's car's headlights cut through the growing darkness, casting long shadows that danced across the gravel path. Olivia sat quietly in the passenger seat, her fingers tracing the edge of the violin case resting against her lap.

Her thoughts churned, caught in a restless tide of questions and fragments of the melody that had burrowed into her mind. The second piece of parchment in her bag felt heavier than it should, its discovery amplifying the sense that they were walking deeper into a web of mystery.

Ahead, the hostel came into view, its silhouette stark against the indigo sky. It wasn't what Olivia had expected, a modest but towering stone building with narrow, arched windows and a steeply pitched roof. The sign above the entrance read St. Brigid's House, the name painted in faded gold script.

"It used to be a convent," Theo said as he turned into the gravel parking lot. "The monks at the monastery recommended it. Said it would be… quiet."

Olivia shot him a skeptical glance. "Quiet is one thing. Haunted is another."

Theo smirked faintly but said nothing, shutting off the engine as they pulled to a stop.

The air outside was cool and damp, carrying the faint scent of earth and woodsmoke. Olivia shivered as she stepped out of the car, the crunch of gravel underfoot breaking the otherwise heavy silence.

The hostel's front door was an imposing wooden slab, its surface weathered and etched with faint carvings of ivy and crosses. Theo knocked twice, the sound echoing faintly in the stillness.

A moment later, the door creaked open, revealing a figure in a black habit. The nun who stood before them was tall and gaunt, her pale face framed by the stark white wimple beneath her veil. Her dark eyes gleamed in the dim light from the doorway, her gaze sharp and assessing.

"Good evening," she said, her voice low and measured, with an accent that carried a faint lilt. "Welcome to St. Brigid's. You must be Mr. Callahan and Ms. Hart."

Olivia felt a shiver run down her spine as the nun said her name, as though she had known it long before Theo made the reservation.

"Yes," Theo said, his tone steady. "We have a booking for two nights."

The nun inclined her head and stepped back, allowing them to enter. As she stepped into the foyer, the scent of beeswax polish and old wood enveloped Olivia. The interior was dimly lit, with a single chandelier casting a warm but muted glow over the stone walls and polished floorboards.

"Follow me," the nun said, her voice echoing softly as she led them down a narrow hallway. Her footsteps were almost soundless, her movements precise and deliberate.

The hallway was lined with faded tapestries depicting saints and biblical scenes, their colors dulled by time. The faint scent of incense lingered in the air, mingling with the earthy aroma of stone.

Their rooms were simple but immaculate. Each was furnished with a narrow bed, a small wooden desk, and a crucifix hanging above the door. The walls were bare stone, and the single window in Olivia's room overlooked the darkened countryside.

Olivia set her bag on the desk and sat on the edge of the bed, her hands resting in her lap. The quiet was almost oppressive, broken only by the occasional creak of the floorboards or the distant murmur of voices from the common area.

There was something about this place, something she couldn't quite name. It wasn't just the stillness or the faint chill in the air. It was a sense of being watched, as though the walls themselves were keeping vigil.

A soft knock on the door startled her, and she looked up to see Theo standing in the doorway.

"Dinner's in half an hour," he said. "You okay?"

Olivia nodded, though her unease lingered. "This place… it feels strange."

Theo leaned against the doorframe, his expression thoughtful. "It's old. Places like this have a lot of history. Sometimes that sticks around."

Olivia swallowed hard and glanced at the violin case by her bag. "Let's just hope it doesn't stick to us."

The dining hall was small and sparsely decorated. Its long wooden table looked like it had been carved from a single massive tree. A cluster of candles flickered at the center of the table, their light casting dancing shadows across the stone walls.

The nun from earlier, Sister Mary, served them bowls of hearty vegetable soup and freshly baked bread. She moved with an otherworldly grace, her dark eyes occasionally flicking toward Olivia as though studying her.

"Is this your first time in Ireland?" Sister Mary asked as she poured tea into Olivia's cup.

"Yes," Olivia replied, her voice quieter than she intended.

The nun nodded, her gaze lingering for a moment before shifting to Theo. "And you? You have the air of someone searching for something."

Theo's expression didn't change, but Olivia noticed the subtle tension in his jaw. "We're following some family history," he said evenly.

Sister Mary smiled faintly. "Ireland is full of stories, though not all of them are kind."

Olivia shivered, feeling the weight of the nun's words settle over her like a shadow.

After dinner, Sister Mary lingered, her gaze fixed on the violin case beside Olivia's chair.

"That instrument," she said, her voice soft but deliberate. "It carries a heavy burden, doesn't it?"

Olivia froze, her fingers tightening around the edge of the table. "What do you mean?"

The nun's expression darkened. "There is a legend, one that speaks of a violin not crafted by human hands. It was said to have been forged by the Devil himself, its strings woven from the hair of the damned."

Theo frowned. "That sounds like folklore."

"Perhaps," Sister Mary said, her tone unchanged. "But every legend is born from a grain of truth. The violin is said to carry a melody that can open doors—doors that should remain closed. Those who play it often see things they cannot explain. And those who seek its secrets rarely return."

Olivia's chest tightened, the melody in her mind swelling to a crescendo. "Have you seen it?" she asked, her voice trembling.

Sister Mary's gaze grew distant. "No. But I have felt its presence."

Sister Mary leaned closer, her dark eyes gleaming in the candlelight as if the fire had sparked them alive. Her voice dropped to a whisper as though sharing the tale would summon the forces she described.

"They say the violin was created as a tool of temptation—a masterpiece of manipulation forged in the darkest depths of hell itself. The Devil, in his cunning, sought to weave something so beautiful, so alluring, that even the most virtuous souls could not resist its call."

Olivia felt her breath hitch, the air in the room suddenly colder.

"The strings," Sister Mary continued, her gaze piercing, "are said to be spun from the hair of the damned, those souls who succumbed to the sin of Pride. It is the deadliest of all sins, you see, for it was Pride that cast Lucifer himself from heaven. And so, the violin was made as both a weapon and a reminder, a perfect instrument, born of the fallen, meant to lure humanity into ruin."

She paused, her fingers resting lightly on the edge of the table. The candlelight flickered, casting long shadows across her face.

"The tormented souls whose hair formed the strings were once celebrated artists, thinkers, and musicians—individuals whose talents shone so brightly that they believed themselves untouchable. They pursued perfection not for the sake of creation but for their own glory. They demanded that the world bow to their genius, and in their arrogance, they ultimately lost their souls."

Olivia's chest tightened, her pulse quickening. She glanced at the violin case beside her, suddenly feeling its weight in the room more acutely than ever.

"Why would the Devil want to create something so beautiful?" Theo asked, his voice steady but low.

Sister Mary's lips curled into a faint smile though it carried no warmth. "Beauty is the most dangerous of all temptations, Mr. Callahan. It blinds us, seduces us, and makes us believe we can control it. The violin was not just an object of beauty—it was a mirror. It reflected the desires of those who touched it, amplified their Pride, and led them to destruction."

She leaned back slightly, folding her hands in her lap. "The melody it plays is incomplete, of course. The Devil ensured it would remain so, for the unfinished melody is the key to its power. Those who hear it are driven to madness, compelled to search for the missing notes. They think they can master it, but the violin truly masters them."

The room seemed to close in around them, the silence heavy with the weight of the story. Olivia's fingers trembled as she reached for her teacup, the liquid now cold and uninviting.

"The melody…" she began, her voice shaking. "It's in my head. It's been there since I touched the violin."

Sister Mary's eyes locked onto hers, sharp and knowing. "Then you must tread carefully, Ms. Hart. The violin is no ordinary instrument. It chooses its players, draws them into its web, and binds them to its will. To hold it, to play it, is to risk your very soul."

Olivia swallowed hard, her throat dry. "And the missing notes? What happens if someone finds them?"

The nun's expression darkened. "If the melody is ever completed, it is said to open a door—a gateway between worlds. Some believe it leads to knowledge and power beyond comprehension, but others… others believe it leads straight to hell."

Sister Mary paused, the weight of the story hanging heavy in the air. She turned her sharp gaze to Theo, her voice dipping even lower as though revealing a part of the tale few had ever heard.

"But there is more," she said, her words deliberate. "The legend does not end with the violin. It is said that the Devil, cunning as he is, did not trust humanity to carry out his plan unsupervised. He sent one of his angels to walk among us, a being born of a union darker than anyone could fathom. The Grim Reaper, as you may know him, is said to have had a first-born son with Mother Time herself. A child created to watch, linger, and witness humanity's descent."

Theo shifted slightly, his jaw tightening as he studied the nun. "What does this… angel do?"

Sister Mary's gaze was unyielding, her tone measured. "His sole purpose is to follow the trail of the violin. Wherever it goes, he is not far behind. He watches those drawn to its melody, who seek to unravel its secrets. He observes how far they are willing to go; how much they are willing to sacrifice."

Olivia felt a chill run through her, and the weight of the violin case by her side was suddenly unbearable. "And then what?" she whispered.

The nun's lips thinned, and her eyes seemed to darken. "If the Grim Reaper's son finds that a human soul has given in fully to the violin's power, if they complete the melody and open the door, it is said that he will be there to claim them. Some say he drags them into the abyss himself. Others believe he simply watches, cold and silent, as they fall into their own ruin."

Theo's voice was calm but edged with suspicion. "Why would the Devil need someone to follow the violin? Isn't the destruction it causes enough?"

Sister Mary tilted her head, her expression unreadable. "The Devil is not just a tempter, Mr. Callahan. He is also a collector. To him, the violin is not just an instrument of chaos; it is a test. It is a way to measure humanity's Pride, greed, and unrelenting thirst for power. And his angel, the Grim Reaper's son, is there to ensure the test is seen through to its end."

A heavy silence fell over the room, the faint crackle of the candles the only sound.

"You're saying… someone could be following us," Olivia said finally, her voice barely above a whisper.

Sister Mary's eyes flicked to the violin case. "If you hold that instrument, Ms. Hart, you can be certain you are not alone. Wherever the violin goes, so does he."

The room seemed colder now, the shadows longer and more oppressive. Olivia's thoughts swirled with the weight of the nun's words, each falling into place like pieces of a puzzle she hadn't realized she was solving.

Theo broke the silence, his voice firm. "Have you ever seen him?"

Sister Mary's gaze lingered on Theo for a long moment, her lips pressing into a thin line. "No," she said softly. "But I have felt his presence. Those who carry the violin often do, whether they realize it or not."

Olivia felt her stomach twist, the edges of her vision narrowing. "What does he look like?"

The nun's eyes softened, but her expression remained grave. "The legends say he appears as a man—ordinary, unremarkable. But you'll know him when you see him. There will be something in his eyes, something that makes you feel as though he sees not just you, but everything you are, everything you've done. You'll hear it in his voice when he speaks: a sharp truth that cuts.

The silence that followed was thick and heavy, broken only by the faint crackle of the candles.

That night, Olivia lay in bed, staring at the ceiling as the nun's words replayed in her mind. The room felt colder than before, the stillness pressing against her like a weight.

She reached for the violin case, her fingers brushing against the leather. The melody, faint but insistent, stirred again, pulling her toward something she couldn't yet see.

As her eyelids grew heavy, she thought she heard faint, soft, melodic, and otherworldly whispers.

Sleep claimed her, but it was anything but restful.

Chapter 10

A DARK PAST RESURFACES

The darkness pressed in from all sides. Olivia stood in a vast, endless void where her breath felt muffled. A flickering golden light appeared in the distance, initially faint but growing stronger and more insistent. She walked toward it, her steps slow and deliberate, though the ground beneath her feet felt as though it didn't exist.

The light resolved into a figure. Tall and cloaked in shadow, the figure stood with an aura of stillness that made her skin prickle. Though his face was obscured, his presence was over-powering—heavy and inescapable.

He held a violin in one hand, its polished wood gleaming un-naturally in the golden light. His other hand rested on the bow, poised as though ready to play, but he didn't move. He simply stood, waiting, his head tilted as if observing her.

Olivia opened her mouth to speak, but no sound came out. Her heart pounded in her chest, each beat echoing in the op-pressive silence.

The figure stepped forward, and the light shifted, illuminat-ing his face, or what should have been his face. Instead, it was a hollow void, a swirling mass of shadow and light that seemed to pull her in.

"Who are you?" Olivia finally managed to whisper, her voice trembling.

His voice was low and resonant when he spoke, cutting through the silence like a blade. "You already know."

She took a step back, her foot catching on something un-seen. The violin in his hand shifted, and for a moment, she thought he would play.

Then he said, "How far will you go, Olivia Hart?"

The melody swelled, loud and haunting, drowning out ev-erything else.

Morning Tension

Olivia woke with a start, her breath coming in short, ragged gasps. The pale light of dawn seeped through the small window of her room, casting long, slanted shadows across the stone walls. Her sheets were damp with sweat, and her hands trembled as she clutched them to her chest.

The dream clung to her like a shroud, vivid and unrelenting. She could still hear the figure's voice and feel the weight of its gaze or lack thereof. It felt so real, more like a memory than a dream, and the question he had asked lingered in her mind like a challenge she couldn't ignore.

"How far will you go?" she whispered to herself, her voice barely audible in the stillness.

Her gaze drifted to the violin case resting against the desk, its dark surface gleaming faintly in the morning light. She felt its presence like a living thing, an unspoken weight in the room.

A knock on the door made her jump.

"Olivia?" Theo's voice was steady but tinged with concern.

"Yeah," she called, her voice hoarse. "I'm coming."

She swung her legs over the side of the bed and stood, her movements slow and deliberate as though the dream had drained her of energy.

When she opened the door, Theo's sharp gaze swept over her. "You look like you've seen a ghost."

"Not quite," Olivia muttered, stepping aside to let him in.

When they arrived, the dining hall was nearly empty, save for Sister Mary and a handful of other guests murmuring quietly over their tea. The long wooden table looked more imposing in the morning light, its surface gleaming with a dull polish.

Olivia barely touched her food, her appetite overshadowed by the lingering unease from the dream. She pushed her eggs around her plate, her gaze unfocused.

"You're quiet," Theo observed, his tone casual but probing.

"Just tired," Olivia replied, though her voice lacked conviction.

Sister Mary approached, her footsteps silent on the stone floor. She placed a small pot of tea on the table and lingered, her sharp gaze settling on Olivia.

"Did you sleep well, Ms. Hart?" she asked, her voice calm but with an edge that sent a shiver down Olivia's spine.

"Not really," Olivia admitted, avoiding the nun's gaze.

Sister Mary nodded, her expression unreadable. "Dreams have a way of revealing truths we do not wish to face."

Theo frowned. "What does that mean?"

The nun smiled faintly, but it didn't reach her eyes. "Only that the violin has its own way of speaking. And sometimes, it chooses the quiet hours of the night to do so."

Olivia's grip tightened around her teacup, her knuckles white. "What if I don't want to hear what it has to say?"

Sister Mary's smile faded. "That is not for you to decide."

After breakfast, they decided to explore the surrounding grounds before leaving for the next leg of their journey. The mist that had settled overnight still clung to the air, wrapping the landscape in a veil of gray.

The small chapel attached to the hostel drew Olivia's attention. Its stained-glass windows glimmered faintly in the muted light, casting fragmented colors onto the damp grass below. She felt an inexplicable pull toward it, her feet moving before her mind could catch up.

Theo followed, his footsteps crunching softly on the gravel path.

The chapel door creaked as Olivia pushed it open, the sound echoing through the empty space. The air inside was cool and heavy, thick with the scent of incense and aged wood. Rows of wooden pews stretched toward the altar, their surfaces worn smooth by years of use.

A statue stood at the front of the chapel, perched on the altar as though it were a silent guardian. It was an angel carved from thick, translucent glass, its delicate wings spread wide, and its head bowed with somber grace. The angel held a violin to its shoulder, the bow frozen mid-stroke as though capturing a moment of eternal performance.

But the most unnerving part of the statue was its base, a large hourglass embedded beneath the angel's feet. The thick, golden sand within was slowly trickling from the top chamber to the bottom, its movement hypnotic. The entire piece had an otherworldly sheen, the glass refracting the faint light from the chapel's windows in strange, shifting patterns.

Olivia froze, her breath catching in her throat. "Theo…"

He stepped beside her, his brow furrowing as he followed her gaze. "What in the world is that?"

She didn't answer immediately. Her eyes were fixed on the base of the hourglass, where an inscription had been etched in flowing, elegant script:

"As time lives, you shall follow."

Olivia's chest tightened, the words seeming to pulse with significance. She took a hesitant step forward, drawn to the statue despite the unease prickling along her skin.

"What do you think it means?" she whispered, her voice barely audible.

Theo shook his head, his expression grim. "It's not a coincidence. This is connected to the violin."

Her fingers hovered above the glass, the smooth surface gleaming like trapped starlight. The sand continued its descent, the faint sound of its fall barely audible, like the ticking of a distant clock.

A sudden rush of cold air swept through the chapel, extinguishing the candles and plunging the room into shadow.

"Olivia, don't," Theo said sharply, grabbing her wrist before her hand could make contact with the statue.

She stumbled back, her breath coming in shallow gasps as the oppressive darkness pressed against her. The faint sound of the sand trickling inside the hourglass now seemed deafening, reverberating through the chapel like a heartbeat.

And then, a voice—low, resonant, and filled with a weight that made her knees buckle.

"You cannot run from what you carry."

The words hung in the air, heavy and final, like a judgment passed.

Theo's grip on her arm tightened. "We need to leave. Now."

Olivia could barely see his outline in the shadows, but his urgency cut through her fear. Together, they stumbled toward the chapel doors, their footsteps echoing in the suffocating silence.

As they burst into the misty morning light, Olivia doubled over, her chest heaving as she struggled to catch her breath. The cold air bit at her skin, but it couldn't chase away the chill that had settled deep in her bones.

"What was that?" she gasped, her voice trembling.

Theo didn't answer immediately. His jaw was tight, his eyes scanning the surrounding area as though expecting someone—or something—to appear.

Finally, he turned to her, his expression dark. "I think we just met your watcher."

Chapter 11

UNRAVELING SECRETS

The mist clung to them as they hurried back to St. Brigid's House, its damp tendrils curling around their clothes and hair. Olivia's breath came in sharp gasps, her heart pounding against her ribs as Theo led the way up the narrow gravel path. The heavy morning silence pressed against her ears, broken only by the crunch of their hurried footsteps and the occasional distant cry of a seabird.

"What the hell was that voice?" Olivia asked, her words spilling out between breaths.

Theo didn't answer immediately, his gaze fixed ahead. He gripped her arm tighter, almost pulling her along.

"I don't know," he said finally, his voice low, "but... I don't think it's done with us."

When they reached the hostel's door, Theo pushed it open with a force that sent the old wood creaking. The warm, familiar scent of beeswax and incense greeted them, but it did nothing to ease the tension that coiled tight in Olivia's chest. They didn't speak as they climbed the stairs, their boots clattering against the stone steps.

Once inside her room, Olivia dropped onto the edge of the bed, her body still trembling from the encounter. The small, simple space suddenly felt too close, the stone walls seeming to lean inward. Her fingers drummed nervously against her knee as her mind raced, replaying the events in the chapel.

The angel, the hourglass, the inscription, "As time lives, you shall follow." Every detail felt deliberate as if it had been waiting for her. But it wasn't just the statue that haunted her. It was the voice, low and resonant, carrying a weight she could still feel in her chest.

She turned to Theo, who leaned against the wall, his arms crossed tightly over his chest. His sharp gaze scanned the room as though expecting something to emerge from the shadows.

"We need to talk to Sister Mary," Olivia said abruptly, breaking the silence.

Theo frowned. "Why? You think she knows what that thing was?"

"I think she knows more than she's letting on," Olivia replied, her voice steady despite the unease twisting in her gut. "The statue, the inscription, this whole place feels like it's part of something bigger. She has to know why."

Theo sighed, running a hand through his hair. "And if she doesn't?"

"Then we keep moving," Olivia said firmly. "But I need answers first."

The hallways of St. Brigid's House were quiet as Olivia and Theo descended the stairs, the faint scent of incense lingering in the air. The soft creak of the floorboards underfoot seemed unnaturally loud, the weight of their thoughts rendering them both silent.

They found Sister Mary in the small dining hall, her tall figure framed by the faint morning light streaming through the narrow windows. She was wiping down a table, her movements slow and deliberate.

"Sister Mary," Olivia said, her voice sharper than she intended.

The nun looked up, her dark eyes settling on them with a calm that seemed unnerving in contrast to the turmoil in Olivia's chest. "Ms. Hart. Mr. Callahan. I see you've been busy."

Olivia stepped closer, her hands clenching into fists at her sides. "You knew, didn't you? About the statue, the voice—everything."

Sister Mary set the cloth down carefully, folding her hands before her. "I told you what I could."

"That's not good enough," Olivia snapped. "There's more to this than you're telling us. What is that statue? What does the inscription mean? And what was that thing we heard in the chapel?"

The nun's calm demeanor faltered for the first time, a shadow passing over her face. She gestured for them to sit at the table, her movements slow and deliberate.

"The statue," she began, her voice quieter than before, "is a relic of the Order of the Hourglass, a sect of monks who believed in the sacred balance of time. They created the statue as a warning, a reminder of what happens when humanity seeks to defy that balance."

Olivia leaned forward, her chest tightening. "Defy it how?"

Sister Mary's gaze fixed on her, unblinking. "Through pride. Ambition. The relentless pursuit of power. The violin is part of this. It was created to tempt, to test, and to corrupt. And those who seek its secrets often find themselves pursued by something far worse than their own greed."

Theo's jaw tightened. "The watcher," he said, his voice low.

The nun inclined her head. "Yes... He is not merely a myth, Mr. Callahan. Wherever the violin goes, he follows. He observes, waits, and ensures that those drawn to its melody face the consequences of their choices."

Olivia's stomach churned. "And the voice we heard in the chapel?"

Sister Mary's lips pressed into a thin line. "If you heard him, Ms. Hart, you are already marked."

The nun's words left Olivia feeling like the ground beneath her had shifted. As she and Theo left the dining hall, the weight of what she had learned settled heavily on her shoulders.

"Marked," she murmured, her voice barely audible.

Theo shot her a sharp glance. "We don't know what that means yet."

"It means we have to keep going," Olivia said, her tone firmer now. "We have to find the rest of the melody. If the violin is a key, then its melody is the lock. Whatever door it opens, we need to find it first."

Theo's brow furrowed, but he didn't argue. Instead, he pulled out the journal and flipped to a page filled with cryptic notes and maps.

"There's another location mentioned here," he said, pointing to a spot on the map. "It's in a small town about two hours from here. It could be our next lead."

Olivia nodded, her resolve hardening. "Then... let's go."

They left St. Brigid's House as the mist began to lift, the sun breaking through in weak, hazy beams. Olivia cast one last glance at the building, its weathered stone walls seeming to watch her as she and Theo climbed into the car.

The road stretched out before them, winding through the rugged Irish countryside. The scent of damp earth and peat smoke lingered in the air, mingling with the faint salty tang of the sea.

As they drove, Olivia stared out the window, her thoughts churning. The watcher, the statue, the violin, every piece of the puzzle felt more ominous than the last. And the inscription, "As time lives, you shall follow," replayed in her mind like a melody she couldn't escape.

She didn't know where the road would lead them next, but one thing was certain: the secrets they were chasing were darker than she had ever imagined, and the violin wasn't done with her yet.

Chapter 12

TENSIONS AND TRUST

The car hummed steadily as Theo drove along the narrow, winding road, the mist rolling over the fields like a ghostly tide. Olivia sat in the passenger seat, absently tracing the edges of the violin case resting on her lap. The earlier encounter in the chapel hung between them, unspoken but heavy.

Theo's knuckles were pale against the steering wheel, his focus locked on the twisting road. The landscape outside was a blur of gray and green, with stone walls and skeletal trees flashing in the dim light.

"You've been quiet," Olivia said finally, breaking the tension.

Theo glanced at her briefly, his expression unreadable. "So have you," he replied.

Olivia sighed, looking out at the mist-shrouded fields. "I just can't stop thinking about what Sister Mary said. About the watcher. About being… marked."

Theo's grip on the wheel tightened. "It doesn't mean we stop," he said firmly. "Whatever this is, we've come too far to turn back now."

Olivia nodded, though her thoughts churned with uncertainty.

The road eventually led them into a small village located in a hollow between rolling hills. It was the kind of place that looked forgotten by time—stone cottages with moss-covered roofs, narrow streets paved with uneven cobblestones, and a pub whose crooked sign swayed gently in the breeze.

Theo parked the car beside the pub, cutting the engine with a decisive key twist.

"Let's stop here for a bit," he said, stepping out before Olivia could respond.

The pub's interior was dimly lit with low wooden beams that seemed to crowd the space. The air smelled faintly of woodsmoke, spilled ale, and damp wool. A few locals sat at the bar, speaking in low tones, their eyes briefly flicking toward Olivia and Theo as they entered.

They sat at a corner table near the fire, which crackled softly in the hearth. Olivia set the violin case on the floor beside her, the leather warm from where she'd been holding it.

"What's the plan now?" she asked.

Theo leaned back in his chair, his gaze distant. "The journal mentions another piece of the melody. We follow that lead."

"And what about the watcher?" Olivia pressed. "What if he's following us?"

Theo's jaw tightened. "Then we stay ahead of him."

Before Olivia could respond, the door to the pub creaked open, and a gust of cold air swept into the room. She and Theo turned toward the entrance, where a man stood silhouetted against the pale light outside.

The man stepped inside, his dark coat hanging loosely from his lean frame. The firelight briefly illuminated his sharp features as he moved further into the room, shaking off the dampness from the mist outside. His hair, streaked with gray at the temples, clung slightly to his forehead, and there was an undeniable air of weariness about him, though his posture was upright and composed.

He made his way to the bar, speaking in low tones to the bartender, who poured him a stout without question. Olivia watched as the man leaned against the counter, his fingers tracing the rim of the glass. He seemed to scan the room, his gray eyes sharp and assessing, though they lingered briefly on her and Theo before continuing their sweep.

Theo shifted in his seat, his fingers tapping a slow rhythm on the table's edge. "He's watching us," he muttered under his breath.

"He's just looking around," Olivia replied, though her voice lacked conviction.

The man took a slow sip of his drink before turning and walking toward their table. His movements were deliberate but unhurried, and as he approached, Olivia felt a strange tension settle over her. He stopped a few feet away, his gaze steady and unreadable.

"Do you mind if I sit?" he asked, his voice smooth, carrying a subtle accent that Olivia couldn't place.

Theo hesitated, his jaw tightening, but Olivia nodded. "Of course," she said, her curiosity outweighing her unease.

The man slid into the empty chair across them, carefully setting his glass down. Up close, Olivia noticed the fine lines around his eyes, etched deep like the grooves of a weathered map. He studied them for a moment, his gray eyes flicking between them.

"Thank you," he said simply. "It's rare to see travelers out here."

"We're just passing through," Theo replied curtly.

"Most are," the man said with a faint smile. "The name's Thebes."

Olivia tilted her head. "Thebes? That's... unusual."

"Unusual is often misunderstood," Thebes replied cryptically, his smile widening just enough to be unsettling.

They talked cautiously at first, Olivia asking safe, surface-level questions while Theo remained guarded. Thebes spoke sparingly, his answers vague but strangely compelling. He claimed to be a traveler who wandered from place to place without a specific destination. Something about the way he spoke, the cadence of his voice, made Olivia feel as though he knew far more than he was saying.

Olivia's gaze drifted toward his neck as they spoke, where a small pendant hung on a thin chain. It was an hourglass. The glass was slightly clouded but still translucent enough to reveal the red substance inside. It wasn't sand; it was thicker, darker, and almost the consistency of blood. It dripped slowly from one chamber to the other, each drop deliberate and measured as though counting moments rather than seconds.

Olivia's breath caught, and she quickly looked away, her mind racing. What kind of person carried something like that? And why?

Theo noticed her distraction and followed her gaze. His eyes narrowed slightly, but he said nothing.

Thebes took another sip of his drink, his gaze flicking toward the window where the mist clung to the glass like a veil. "The road has a way of calling to certain people," he said softly, almost to himself.

"What do you mean?" Olivia asked, her voice barely above a whisper.

Thebes smiled again, though it didn't reach his eyes. "You feel it, don't you? That pull. The need to keep moving, to find something just out of reach."

Neither Theo nor Olivia responded, but the silence that followed seemed to confirm his words.

By the time they finished their drinks, it was clear Thebes had no intention of staying in the village. When he asked if they could give him a ride to the next town, Olivia hesitated, glancing at Theo for guidance. His expression was unreadable, but after a moment, he nodded.

"Fine," Theo said. "We're heading that way anyway."

Thebes inclined his head in gratitude, his gray eyes glinting faintly in the firelight. "You're very kind."

The car moved steadily along the narrow, winding road, its headlights cutting through the mist that had thickened with the evening. The atmosphere inside was heavy, the silence stretching like an invisible thread between them. Theo gripped the steering wheel tightly, his gaze fixed on the road ahead. Olivia sat in the passenger seat, her hands resting on the violin case in her lap, her fingers occasionally drumming against the worn leather.

Thebes sat in the backseat, his presence almost unnervingly still. He leaned slightly against the door, his face half-lit by the dim glow of the dashboard lights. He hadn't spoken since they'd left the pub, and somehow, the absence of his voice was louder than any conversation could have been.

The silence wasn't comfortable; it carried weight, an unspoken tension that neither Theo nor Olivia could ignore. The sound of the car's engine filled the void, steady and low, accompanied by the occasional rustle of wind against the windows.

Olivia couldn't bring herself to look back at Thebes, though she felt his presence keenly. He was there, just behind her, and even though he said nothing, she couldn't shake the feeling that he was studying them, quietly observing every detail.

The mist outside clung to the countryside, shrouding the trees and hills in an eerie haze. The world beyond the car seemed distant, almost unreal as if they were driving through a space that existed outside of time.

Theo shifted slightly, his knuckles pale against the steering wheel. Olivia noticed the tension in his posture, the way his shoulders seemed locked in place. She wanted to say something to break the silence, but the weight of it pressed down on her chest, leaving her unsure of what to say or if she even should.

A faint sound, perhaps a soft sigh, came from the backseat. Olivia glanced at the rearview mirror and saw Thebes's face, illuminated faintly by the passing light. His expression was calm, but there was an intensity in his gray eyes that made her stomach twist. She looked away quickly, her gaze returning to the endless ribbon of road ahead.

The silence remained unbroken, stretching with every mile they traveled. It wasn't awkward or absentminded quiet; it was deliberate and purposeful, as though Thebes wanted them to feel it, and... they did.

When Theo finally slowed the car and pulled to a stop at a crossroads, Olivia exhaled a breath she hadn't realized she'd been holding.

"This is where I get off," Thebes said, his voice low and steady. It was the first time he'd spoken since they'd left, and his voice felt almost startling after the long silence.

Theo nodded stiffly, saying nothing as Thebes opened the door and stepped out into the mist.

The spot was marked by an ancient oak tree, its twisted branches reaching skyward like skeletal fingers. The ground beneath the tree was worn smooth, as though countless travelers had paused there before continuing their journey.

Olivia turned to say something, perhaps to ask him about the hourglass pendant, but the words died on her lips as Thebes reached into his pocket and withdrew a small object.

"For your trouble," he said, holding his hand through the crack of Olivia's window.

Theo hesitated before taking it, his fingers brushing against Thebes's cool skin. The object was a heavy and golden coin, its surface etched with intricate, swirling symbols. It shimmered faintly in the dim light, almost as if alive.

"What's this for?" Theo asked.

Thebes smiled faintly, his gray eyes glinting. "You'll know when the time comes."

Before they could ask another question, Thebes turned and walked away, his coat billowing slightly in the breeze. He disappeared into the mist without a sound, leaving Olivia and Theo stunned.

Theo turned the coin over in his hand

"What the hell just happened?"

"I don't know," Olivia murmured, her gaze fixed on the spot where Thebes had vanished. "But he wasn't just some hitchhiker."

Theo nodded slowly, his eyes narrowing as he examined the coin. "This feels… significant."

They sat silently for a long moment, the weight of the encounter settling heavily over them. Olivia couldn't shake the image of Thebes's hourglass pendant, the thick red liquid dripping slowly within it. It felt like a warning, a reminder of the time slipping away from them.

Somehow, she knew their paths hadn't crossed by chance. Thebes was part of this, just as much as the violin, the watcher, and the melody that continued to haunt her thoughts.

And somewhere in the distance, she could almost hear that haunting tune rising once more.

Chapter 13

THE MEMORY
AT THE SEA

The car rumbled quietly as it idled on the side of the road, its headlights barely cutting through the dense mist that had gathered around them. Olivia sat in the passenger seat, her fingers nervously tapping against the violin case on her lap. The weight of the golden coin Theo now held seemed to fill the car, though it was small enough to fit in his palm.

Theo turned the coin over slowly, his brow furrowed. The faint symbols etched into its surface shimmered in the dim light of the dashboard. "This isn't just a token," he murmured.

Olivia's gaze remained fixed on the mist beyond the windshield. "No. It's a message. Or a… piece of something bigger."

Theo slipped the coin into his pocket with a sharp motion, breaking the moment. "We need to keep moving. Sitting here isn't going to get us anywhere."

He shifted the car back into gear, and they pulled away from the crossroads, the gravel crunching beneath the tires.

The landscape beyond the windows blurred into shades of gray and green, the countryside shrouded in a mist that seemed thicker than before. The winding road curved sharply, bordered by low stone walls and the occasional gnarled tree that stood like a sentinel against the gloom.

Neither Theo nor Olivia spoke, the silence between them tense and uneasy. The faint hum of the engine was their only companion, a steady rhythm that underscored the weight of their thoughts.

Olivia's mind churned with fragments of the past few hours: the stranger's enigmatic presence, the dripping hourglass pendant around his neck, and the haunting tone of his voice when he'd said, "You'll know when the time comes."

She shivered involuntarily and hugged the violin case closer to her chest, the leather cool and solid beneath her fingertips.

Theo's voice broke the silence, low and edged with tension. "The journal mentioned something about the coast. Do you remember?"

Olivia blinked, pulling herself from her thoughts. "Yeah," she said slowly. "A seaside village. It said there might be another piece of the melody there."

Theo nodded, his grip on the wheel tightening. "That has to be where we're headed."

Olivia leaned back in her seat, her gaze drifting to the side window. The mist pressed against the glass, turning the world outside into a blurred, shifting canvas. Somewhere in the distance, she thought she heard the faint sound of waves, a rhythmic crash that seemed to echo in her chest.

By the time they reached the village, the mist had begun to lift, revealing a quiet, weathered place perched on the sea's edge. The cobbled streets wound through clusters of stone cottages, their roofs dark with moss and their windows glowing faintly with the golden light of oil lamps. The salty tang of the ocean filled the air, carried on a brisk wind that tugged at Olivia's hair as she stepped out of the car.

Theo parked near the edge of the village, where the cobblestones gave way to a narrow dirt path that led toward the cliffs. The sound of the sea was louder now, crashing against the rocks below with a force that sent a fine spray of saltwater into the air.

"This place feels… ancient," Olivia murmured, her voice barely audible over the wind.

Theo nodded, his sharp gaze scanning the village. "Let's find somewhere to stay for the night. We'll figure out our next move in the morning."

The inn they found was a small, unassuming building tucked between two larger cottages. Its wooden sign, carved with the words The Anchor's Rest, creaked faintly in the wind as they approached.

Inside, the air was warm and smelled faintly of smoke and brine. The innkeeper, a stout woman with kind eyes and a weathered face, greeted them from behind the counter.

"Long way from home, aren't you?" she said, her voice tinged with curiosity as she handed Theo a key.

"We're just passing through," Theo replied smoothly.

The woman nodded but didn't press further. "Room's at the end of the hall," she said, gesturing toward the narrow corridor that led deeper into the inn. "Breakfast's at dawn if you're up for it."

As Theo pocketed the key, Olivia hesitated, her gaze lingering on the woman. There was something about her—an air of quiet knowing, as though she could see more than what was on the surface.

"Have you lived here long?" Olivia asked, her voice cautious.

The innkeeper smiled faintly. "Long enough to know every crack in these walls and every whisper of the sea."

Olivia hesitated, then decided to press on. "Have you ever heard of a violin? An old one with a strange melody?"

The woman's smile faltered, and her gaze darkened slightly. She leaned forward, her voice dropping to a near whisper. "You'll want to be careful asking questions like that around here."

"Why?" Theo asked, his tone sharp.

The woman glanced toward the window, where the wind rattled faintly against the panes. Her voice dropped, carrying a weight that made Olivia lean in to hear. "The sea always washes its secrets to the shore," she said slowly, her eyes distant, "but the earth holds them tight—at Houska Castle."

Olivia's brow furrowed, her heart skipping a beat at the name. "Houska Castle? That's… that's a day away," she said, her voice tinged with disbelief.

The woman turned back to her, her gaze piercing and steady. "You've already started the clock," she said, her tone quiet but firm. "Waiting or distance are trivial concepts when time catches up to you."

Olivia felt a chill run down her spine, the words settling heavily in her chest like stones. She exchanged a glance with Theo, who was now gripping the key to their room tightly in his hand, his expression grim but unreadable.

"Time's catching up to us?" Olivia whispered, almost to herself.

The woman didn't respond. She simply turned and began to tidy the counter, her movements deliberate, as though the conversation had already ended.

That night, Olivia couldn't sleep. She lay on the narrow bed, staring at the dark ceiling as the waves filled her ears.

Eventually, she rose and crossed to the window, pushing it open slightly. The cold sea air rushed in, sharp and bracing, carrying the faint scent of salt and kelp. She rested her hands on the windowsill, her gaze drifting toward the distant cliffs.

The waves crashed relentlessly against the rocks below, their rhythm almost hypnotic. As she watched, the melody returned—not faint and fleeting like before, but clear and insistent, as though it were being carried on the wind.

Her vision blurred, and the world around her seemed to shift. Suddenly, she was no longer standing at the window but on the edge of the cliffs, the wind tearing at her hair and clothes. The endless and dark sea stretched out before her, its surface gleaming faintly under a pale moon. And there, standing at the edge of the water, was a figure; It was Thebes.

He stood motionless, his coat billowing slightly in the wind. Around his neck, the hourglass pendant gleamed faintly, the red liquid within dripping slowly, methodically, from one chamber to the other.

Olivia took a step toward him, her heart pounding. "What do you want?" she called, her voice lost in the roar of the waves.

Thebes turned his head slowly, his gray eyes locking onto hers. "The melody is waiting," he said, his voice carrying easily over the distance. "But so is the sea."

Olivia frowned, her confusion growing. "The innkeeper said the earth holds the secrets at Houska Castle. Is that where we need to go?"

Thebes raised his hand, pointing past the cliffs and toward the horizon. A faint golden light flickered in the distance, hazy and unreachable.

"Houska Castle is not a destination," he said, his voice resonating in her chest. "It is a mirror, a place where the past, present, and future meet. But the melody will guide you, and the clock is already ticking. Do not waste it. "

The waves surged higher, crashing against the rocks with a force that sent spray flying into the air. Thebes's image flickered like a flame caught in the wind.

"Follow it," he said, his voice softer now but no less urgent. "Before time runs out. The watcher will continue to guide you."

The vision dissolved, leaving Olivia alone at the window. Her breath came in short, sharp gasps. The melody still played faintly in her mind, the rhythm of the waves blending with its haunting refrain.

When dawn broke, Olivia and Theo stood on the cliffs, the salty wind tugging at their jackets. The village was silent behind them; only the distant cries of seabirds and the constant crash of the waves below broke the stillness.

Theo adjusted the strap of his bag, his sharp gaze fixed on the horizon. "So, Houska Castle," he said, his voice calm but firm. "The innkeeper made it sound like that's where everything leads. You had the same feeling, didn't you?"

Olivia nodded, her hands tightening around the violin case. "Thebes said it's where time and silence converge. He called it a mirror; something about the past, present, and future meeting there."

Theo's expression darkened. "That lines up with what we've been seeing. The visions, the watcher, the melody; it's all tied to that place. But it's not close. We're looking at a full day's drive."

"We don't have time to worry about that," Olivia said firmly. "The clock's already ticking."

Theo tilted his head slightly, his gaze lingering on her. "And you're sure about this?"

Olivia glanced at the waves, the memory of Thebes's warning echoing in her mind. "I'm sure," she said, her voice steady. "We can't stop now."

Theo nodded, his jaw tightening. "Alright. Then let's move."

They turned toward the car, their steps brisk and purposeful. Olivia cast one last glance at the cliffs, the faint golden light from her vision seeming to shimmer just beyond the edge of her sight.

The path ahead was clear now, but the journey to Houska Castle promised to be anything but straightforward.

Chapter 14

DOUBT

The car rumbled steadily along the narrow road, the mist clinging to the hills like a shroud. Olivia sat silently in the passenger seat, her hands resting on the violin case in her lap. Her thoughts were tangled; the past few days' events created a web of questions and unease that she couldn't unravel.

Theo was focused on the road, his expression calm but distant. His fingers tapped lightly against the steering wheel, a steady rhythm filling the quiet. For the first time since this journey began, the silence between them felt suffocating.

Olivia turned to him, studying his profile—the sharp line of his jaw, the faint crease between his brows. He had been steady and reliable from the start, but she now realized how little she knew about him. Who was Theo, really?

The question had been simmering at the back of her mind for days, but now, in the confined space of the car, it felt impossible to ignore. She glanced at the golden coin resting in the cupholder between them, its strange symbols catching the dim light. Her thoughts drifted to the stories she had heard about the watcher, the one who follows the trail of the violin, testing those who dared to pursue it.

The cryptic warning echoed in her mind: "You cannot run from what you carry."

Her pulse quickened as a troubling thought surfaced. What if Theo wasn't just helping her? What if he was part of this?

The idea felt absurd, but the more she thought about it, the harder it was to dismiss. Theo had appeared so suddenly in her life, offering to help without hesitation. He knew so much about the violin, about her father's work. And then there were the coincidences—the way he always seemed to know where to go, what to do.

She swallowed hard, her chest tightening. What if Theo was the watcher?

Theo glanced at her, breaking the silence. "You've been quiet," he said, his voice even.

Olivia forced a smile, though her throat felt tight. "Just… thinking."

He nodded, his gaze returning to the road. "About what?"

For a moment, she didn't answer. Her heart was racing now, her breaths coming shallow and fast. She clenched her hands around the violin case, trying to steady herself.

"About you," she said, her voice barely above a whisper.

Theo's brow furrowed, but he didn't look at her. "What about me?"

Olivia hesitated, unsure how to put her swirling thoughts into words. "You've been helping me this whole time, but… I don't know why. I don't really know anything about you, Theo."

He exhaled sharply, his fingers tightening on the wheel. "I guess I haven't given you much reason to trust me," he admitted.

"No, you have," Olivia said quickly, though her chest felt caving in. "It's just… you've sacrificed so much to help me. I don't understand why you care so much about this… About me."

Theo's jaw tightened, and for a long moment, he said nothing. The silence in the car grew heavier, pressing down on Olivia like a weight.

Finally, with a calm but firm voice, Theo said, "I had a good life before this—a wife, a career I loved, and a plan for the future. Then I worked on that violin."

Olivia's breath hitched, but she didn't interrupt.

"I previously shared that I lived in Vienna and worked for Klaus," Theo continued. "However, I didn't tell you what happened after I met your father. Once I came into contact with the violin, my wife, Eleanor, began to fall ill around the same time we started working on it. At first, she experienced minor issues like headaches and fatigue, but her condition deteriorated quickly. The doctors couldn't find anything wrong, but I knew... I knew it was the violin. It felt as though it was draining the life out of her."

Olivia shivered, and the air in the car felt suddenly colder. "What happened to her?"

Theo's grip on the wheel tightened. "She recovered—slowly—after the violin left the shop. But it took a toll on her and on us. By the time it was over, I couldn't look at another violin without thinking about what this instrument had almost cost me.

He glanced at her briefly, his expression serious. "That's why I'm here, Olivia. Your dad trusted me to work on the violin. When I discovered that you are his daughter, I knew I couldn't walk away, not after everything that's happened."

Theo's words hung in the air, but Olivia's mind was racing. His story was tragic, but it didn't ease the gnawing doubt in her chest. If anything, it only deepened it.

Her hands trembled as she gripped the violin case tighter. She tried to focus on the road ahead, but the unease wouldn't let her go. What if Theo's connection to the violin was more than coincidence? What if he hadn't just restored it but had been marked by it?

She remembered Thebes's hourglass pendant, the slow, steady drip of red liquid that felt like time was slipping away. She also thought of Theo's watchful gaze, his knowledge of the violin, and his presence in her life at exactly the right moment.

Her breathing grew shallow, her chest tightening as panic threatened to overwhelm her.

"Olivia?" Theo's voice cut through her spiraling thoughts, sharp with concern.

She blinked, realizing that her vision had blurred and her hands were trembling visibly. "I'm fine," she said quickly, though her voice betrayed her.

"You're not fine," Theo said firmly, pulling the car over to the side of the road. He turned to face her, his gray eyes searching hers. "What's going on?"

Olivia shook her head, trying to steady herself. "I just… I need a minute."

Theo didn't press her, but his gaze remained fixed on her, steady and unyielding.

Olivia forced herself to think logically as she sat there, trying to catch her breath. Theo had been with her from the beginning. He had risked everything to help her, leaving his life behind for a journey without guarantees.

But the doubt lingered like a shadow that wouldn't be shaken.

Finally, she looked at him, her voice trembling. "Theo… why did you really come with me? Was it just for my dad? Or is there something you're not telling me?"

Theo's expression darkened, his jaw tightening. "I came because it's the right thing to do, Olivia. Because your father believed in something that was bigger than himself. And because… maybe I owe him. But that's it."

Olivia nodded slowly, but the unease didn't fully dissipate.

They drove in silence after that, the tension between them palpable but unspoken. Olivia stared out the window, her thoughts racing, the misty landscape blurring into shades of gray.

She wanted to believe Theo; she needed to believe him. But as the haunting melody played faintly in her mind, she couldn't shake the feeling that there was more to his story.

And somewhere deep inside, she feared the truth would change everything.

Chapter 15

IN THE SHADOWS

The darkness of the forest pressed against the car as it wound through narrow, twisting roads. The headlights sliced through the mist, revealing fleeting glimpses of skeletal trees clawing at the sky. Inside the car, Olivia clutched the violin case tightly, her knuckles white against the leather.

She had dozed off earlier, but the nightmare still clung to her like a shadow. In the dream, she stood at the edge of a vast, black pit. The ground crumbled beneath her feet as whispers rose from the depths, voices that were too low to understand but filled with a terrible urgency.

She blinked, trying to shake the memory, but the echo of the dream lingered.

"You okay?" Theo's voice broke through her thoughts.

She glanced at him, noting the tension in his jaw as he focused on the road. "I'm fine," she lied, though her heart was still pounding.

As they rounded a sharp bend, the mist seemed to part, and Houska Castle materialized before them like a specter.

Olivia's breath caught as the castle loomed into view. It wasn't just the size of the structure—though it was massive, its Gothic spires clawing at the sky—it was the oppressive weight of its presence.

The ancient stone walls were blackened with age, the surface cracked and weathered as if bearing the scars of a battle against time. Hundreds of windows stared down at them, dark and empty, like the hollow sockets of a skull. A shiver ran down her spine, and she instinctively clutched the violin case tighter.

Theo guided the car through a rusted iron gate that groaned like a tortured soul. Gravel crunched beneath the tires as they rolled to a stop in the courtyard. For a moment, neither of them moved. The air was unnaturally still, the silence so complete it felt suffocating.

"Welcome to Houska Castle," Theo said, his voice low.

Olivia nodded, though her stomach churned with unease. Before they could step out of the car, the sound of deliberate footsteps echoed through the courtyard. Olivia's head snapped toward the castle's entrance, where a tall, lean figure emerged from the shadows.

The man was older, his silver hair slicked back, his sharp features illuminated by the weak light. He wore a dark coat that flared slightly in the wind, and his piercing eyes seemed to take in everything at once.

"You must be Olivia and Theo," he said, his voice smooth and accented, though Olivia couldn't place it.

Theo stepped forward, his expression wary. "You must be Marek."

The man inclined his head. "I am. And you are just in time. The castle has been waiting."

Marek led them through the heavy wooden doors, which creaked on their hinges as they opened. The air inside was colder, carrying the scent of damp stone and something faintly metallic. Shadows pooled in the corners of the vast entry hall, their shapes shifting as if alive.

Olivia's boots clicked softly against the worn stone floor as she followed Marek. Her eyes darted to the faded tapestries hanging on the walls, their once-vivid colors dulled by centuries of decay. One depicted a cloaked figure standing over a pit, holding a violin in one hand and a burning torch in the other.

"What is this place?" she asked, her voice barely above a whisper.

"Houska Castle was built to contain a great evil," Marek replied, his tone matter-of-fact. "The pit beneath the chapel is said to be a gateway to Hell itself. The castle was not constructed to keep invaders out but to keep what lies within from escaping."

As they moved deeper into the castle, the oppressive atmosphere thickened. Cold spots lingered in the air, and Olivia swore she heard faint whispers coming from the walls.

Marek stopped abruptly in a narrow hallway, his hand brushing against a tapestry. He pulled it aside to reveal a hidden door, its wood warped and splintered with age.

"Through here," he said, his voice low.

Theo exchanged a glance with Olivia before nodding. Marek pushed the door open, and they descended a narrow spiral staircase. The further they went, the colder it became, the air growing damp and heavy.

When they reached the bottom, Marek gestured toward a large stone slab carved with intricate runes that seemed to shimmer faintly in the dim light. Markings similar to those on the coin that Thebes had provided to them were visible on the stone.

"This is the pit," he said. "It has been sealed for centuries, but its power still seeps through."

Olivia stepped closer, her breath catching. The runes seemed to pulse faintly, as if alive.

"What happens if the seal is broken?" Theo asked, his voice tight.

Marek's expression darkened. "If the seal is broken, the creatures of the pit will be free to roam the earth. The violin is one of the few things that can open it."

Marek turned to Olivia, his gaze piercing. "The violin was crafted from the wood of a tree that grew near this pit. Its strings are said to be made from the hair of the damned. It carries with it the power of the pit, and its melody can either strengthen the seal or destroy it."

Olivia's grip on the violin case tightened. "Why would anyone create something like that?"

Marek's lips pressed into a thin line. "It was not created by human hands. The violin is a tool of the devil, meant to tempt and test. It reveals the truth of those who play it, their desires, fears, and weaknesses."

Theo's jaw tightened. "And what about the watcher?"

Marek's gaze flicked to Theo, his expression unreadable. "The watcher exists to ensure the violin does not fall into the wrong hands. It observes, judges, and, if necessary, intervenes."

Olivia felt a chill run down her spine. "Intervenes, how?"

Marek didn't answer, his eyes lingering on Theo for a moment too long.

As they turned to leave, a low, rumbling sound echoed through the chamber. Olivia froze, her heart racing as the runes on the stone slab began to glow brighter.

"What's happening?" she whispered.

"The pit is stirring," Marek said, his voice tense. "It knows the violin is near."

Theo placed a hand on Olivia's shoulder, guiding her back toward the stairs. "We need to go."

As they ascended, Olivia couldn't shake the feeling that the shadows were moving, reaching for them. The whispers grew louder, and for a moment, she thought she heard her name.

When they finally emerged into the chapel, Olivia turned to Marek. "What are we supposed to do?"

Marek's gaze was steady, but his voice was grave. "You must decide whether the violin's power is worth the risk. But know this: once the seal is broken, there is no turning back."

As they left the chapel, Olivia's mind raced. The violin wasn't just a tool but a weapon, a key to unimaginable power. And yet, she couldn't shake the feeling that Theo's connection to it was deeper than he let on.

She glanced at him, her chest tightening as his calm demeanor unsettled her. Was he just here to help her, or was there something more to his presence?

The words of the watcher echoed in her mind: "You cannot run from what you carry."

And for the first time, Olivia wondered if the heaviness she felt came not just from the violin, but from the truth about Theo as well.

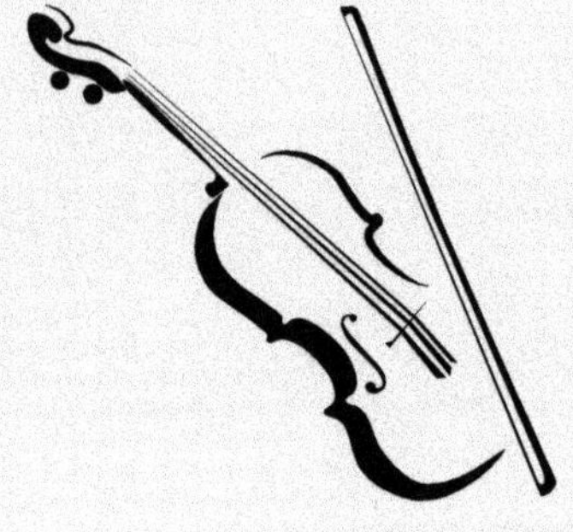

Chapter 16

THE CURSE REVEALED

The castle's air grew heavier as Olivia followed Marek through the dimly lit halls. The stone walls seemed to absorb sound, muffling even the faintest creak of her boots against the floor. Every shadow seemed to shift when she wasn't looking, the flickering torchlight casting shapes that danced like restless spirits.

"This way," Marek said, his voice echoing slightly in the narrow corridor.

Olivia glanced back at Theo, who walked behind her, his expression unreadable. The weight of everything they'd learned so far pressed down on her chest, making it hard to breathe.

They stopped in front of a heavy wooden door. Marek pushed it open, revealing a modest room with two beds and a small fireplace. The faint scent of damp stone lingered in the air.

"You'll stay here for the night," Marek said, his eyes lingering on Olivia for a moment longer than she liked. "The castle... has a way of revealing truths to those who enter it. Rest, but be vigilant."

"Revealing truths?" Theo asked, his tone sharp.

Marek didn't answer. He merely inclined his head and slipped back into the shadows, leaving them alone.

Once the door shut, Olivia pulled out her rosary, the familiar touch of the beads grounding her. She slipped it around her neck, the cross resting lightly against her chest.

"What are you doing?" Theo asked, his voice low.

"Something feels... wrong here," she admitted, her fingers brushing over the rosary. "The air feels heavy like it's pressing down on me. I can't explain it."

Theo's gaze softened slightly, but he said nothing. Instead, he sat on the edge of one of the beds, staring into the small, empty fireplace.

Olivia paced the room, her unease growing with every passing moment. She couldn't shake the feeling that they were being watched, that something unseen lingered just beyond the edge of her perception.

Finally, exhaustion overtook her, and she lay down. Despite the rosary's comforting presence, sleep did not come easily.

Olivia opened her eyes to find herself standing in an unfamiliar garden. The air was thick and humid, carrying a faint metallic scent that made her stomach churn. The sky above was a dull gray, devoid of sunlight or stars, casting an eerie glow over the landscape.

The garden was unlike anything she had ever seen. The trees were tall and twisted, their bark dark and slick, like wet stone. The stems and branches resembled human blood vessels, intertwining in grotesque, organic patterns. A crimson liquid pulsed slowly inside the translucent bark, moving like blood through veins.

She stepped forward, her boots sinking slightly into the damp, spongy ground. A low hum filled the air, a sound that seemed to come from the trees themselves.

"Olivia," a voice called softly.

She turned to see a woman standing at the edge of the garden. Her figure was shrouded in a pale, ethereal glow, and her long, dark hair flowed like water around her shoulders. Her face was strikingly familiar, though Olivia couldn't place it.

"Who are you?" Olivia asked, her voice trembling.

The woman smiled faintly, her eyes filled with both warmth and sadness. "I am someone who knows your family's story better than anyone. Come, I'll show you."

The woman led Olivia deeper into the garden, the trees growing denser and grotesque with every step. The pulsing liquid inside their stems seemed to glow faintly now, casting an eerie red light.

"What is this place?" Olivia asked, her voice barely above a whisper.

"This is the garden of curses," the woman replied. "Every tree here represents a legacy of pain, a lineage marked by darkness. And this…" She gestured to a particularly large and gnarled tree. "This is your family's tree."

Olivia stared at the tree, her breath catching in her throat. The bark was darker than the others, and the liquid inside pulsed more violently as though the tree was alive and angry.

"This… this can't be real," she said, taking a step back.

"It is as real as the curse that binds your bloodline," the woman said, her voice steady. "It began generations ago when one of your ancestors struck a bargain with forces they did not understand."

"What kind of bargain?" Olivia asked, her voice shaking.

The woman placed a hand on the tree, her fingers sinking slightly into the bark as though it were flesh. "Your ancestor sought power—something extraordinary, something that would outlast them," the woman said, her voice heavy with regret. "But the violin wasn't crafted by them. It was born of the pit itself, shaped by Satan's hand. When your ancestors entered the pact, they were lured to the cursed tree growing near the pit. Satan promised them that the violin would bring them the greatness they sought and that its music would captivate the world. But he didn't tell them that the violin would also carry the darkness of the pit, a fragment of Hell itself. It became a vessel of his will, bound to your family's bloodline as both a tool and a punishment."

Olivia felt her stomach twist. "So the violin… it's tied to my family?"

The woman nodded solemnly. "It carries more than the ambitions of your ancestor. It carries the weight of their pact and the curse that has plagued your bloodline ever since."

Olivia's breath hitched. "What curse?"

The woman gestured toward the garden's twisted trees, their blood-like sap pulsing violently. "Your ancestor bound your family to the violin when they agreed to serve its purpose. That purpose is nearing its end, and the curse will demand a final price. The melody your father was trying to finish—it's not just music; It's a key. When completed, it will open the pit and unleash the darkness within."

Olivia staggered back, her legs trembling. "And if it's destroyed?"

The woman's gaze darkened. "To destroy the violin is to sever the pact, but the severing requires a sacrifice. Someone of your bloodline must take its place to keep the pit sealed."

"What does that mean?" Olivia whispered, though she already feared the answer.

The woman's voice softened, tinged with sorrow. "You would become the gatekeeper, bound to the pit for eternity."

Olivia sank to her knees, her mind spinning. "Why didn't my dad tell me this? Why didn't he warn me?"

"He tried to protect you," the woman said gently. "But the violin calls to those it marks. He knew you would hear it someday, no matter how hard he tried to shield you. The curse finds its way, Olivia. It always does."

The trees around them seemed to pulse with the rhythm of her racing heartbeat, the crimson liquid within their stems bubbling furiously.

"There has to be another way," Olivia pleaded, her voice cracking.

The woman stood, her glowing figure starting to fade into the garden's shadows. "There is no other way," she said. "But the choice will be yours. Destroy the violin and bind yourself to the pit, or finish the melody and let the world bear the cost."

Her final words echoed as she disappeared into the crimson-tinged fog: "Time is running out."

Olivia woke with a start, her heart pounding as though she'd been running. The faint glow of the fire cast long, jagged shadows across the stone walls. She reached instinctively for the rosary around her neck, gripping the beads as if they were the only solid thing in a crumbling world.

She couldn't shake the dream, the cursed garden, the woman's ominous warning, and the impossible choice that now loomed before her.

Theo stirred in the other bed, his gray eyes opening slowly to find her sitting upright, clutching the rosary. "What's wrong?" he asked, groggy but concerned.

"Just a bad dream," Olivia said, her voice barely steady.

Theo sat up, his sharp gaze lingering on her. "You've been having a lot of those."

She hesitated, the weight of the truth pressing down on her chest. "It doesn't matter," she said quietly. "I need to finish what my ancestors started."

Olivia remained sitting as Theo lay back down, staring at the faintly glowing embers in the fireplace.

The woman's words echoed in her mind, louder and more insistent now: Time is running out.

Chapter 17

THE MELODY

The morning after Olivia's dream carried an unsettling silence as though the castle itself was waiting. She sat on the edge of her bed, the violin case resting heavily at her feet. The rosary around her neck felt strangely warm against her skin, as though it were trying to shield her from the decision she knew she had to make.

Her dream had been vivid, too vivid to dismiss. The garden of curses, the woman's haunting words, and the weight of generations pulling her toward an impossible choice. She couldn't shake the memory of the final warning: Time is running out.

Theo leaned against the cold stone wall, watching her closely. His face betrayed little emotion, but his fingers drummed absently against his folded arms, a small crack in his composure.

"Are you ready?" he asked, his voice low and steady yet tinged with something she couldn't quite place.

"No," Olivia replied, standing anyway. She slipped the strap of the violin case over her shoulder and adjusted the rosary. Her hands trembled as she tightened the strap, betraying the confidence she was trying to project.

Theo straightened, nodding once. He didn't press her or offer reassurances. They both knew there was no certainty in what lay ahead.

Marek led them through the narrow corridors of Houska Castle, his lantern casting flickering light across the damp stone walls. The air grew colder the deeper they descended, thick and heavy with an energy that pressed down on Olivia's chest.

She tried to focus on the rhythm of her footsteps and the scrape of her boots against the uneven floor, but the faint hum of the violin against her back pulled her attention. Its vibrations were subtle, but she could feel them resonating with something deep below.

Theo walked beside her, his presence steady, but his silence felt heavier than usual. Olivia's gaze flickered to the hourglass pendant hanging around his neck. The crimson liquid inside dripped slowly, its steady rhythm an unspoken reminder of how little time they had left.

Her stomach churned. She hadn't seen Theo receive the pendant, but there it was, a relic of Thebes, now inexplicably his. The thought gnawed at her, planting seeds of doubt.

They descended a spiraling staircase, the air growing colder with each step. The walls seemed to close in around them, and the faint sound of dripping water echoed eerily in the silence.

At last, they emerged into a vast underground chamber. The walls were carved directly into the rock, lined with glowing runes that pulsed faintly like a heartbeat. At the center of the room, a jagged black pit yawned open, its edges raw and uneven as though the earth had been ripped apart.

The darkness within the pit wasn't empty; it swirled faintly, alive with movement. A low hum emanated from it, resonating with the vibrations of the violin. Olivia couldn't tear her eyes away, her breath catching in her throat.

"The gateway," Marek said, his voice solemn.

Olivia took a hesitant step forward, the pull of the pit stronger than she had anticipated. The darkness seemed to whisper her name, a sound she couldn't block out.

"Olivia," Theo's voice cut through her thoughts, grounding her. But she no longer trusted him.

Marek gestured toward a stone pedestal near the edge of the pit. Resting atop it was a weathered sheet of parchment, its edges curled and singed. Olivia didn't need to read the notes to know what it was the final piece of the melody.

She stepped toward it slowly, her heart pounding. The violin case vibrated more insistently now, its hum deep and mournful, resonating in her chest like a second heartbeat.

"The melody, when completed, will unlock the gateway," Marek said. "And release everything within it."

Olivia reached for the parchment, her hand trembling as her fingers brushed its surface. The notes were intricate and haunting, etched in dark ink that seemed to shimmer faintly in the lantern light.

"You don't have to do this," Theo said, stepping closer. His voice was steady, but she caught a flicker of desperation in his eyes.

She looked up at him, searching his face for answers. "Don't I?"

Theo opened his mouth to respond, but Marek interrupted, his voice cold and unyielding.

"She must choose. Finish the melody and unleash the pit, or destroy the violin and seal it forever. But beware...destroying the violin will bind her to the gateway. She will become its guardian."

Olivia ignored the warning and turned to Theo. Her gaze caught on the hourglass pendant around his neck again, and her breath hitched. The crimson liquid inside dripped rhythmically, each drop a silent confirmation of what she had feared.

"How do you have that?" she demanded, her voice shaking.

Theo froze, his expression unreadable. "Olivia..."

"You've been watching me," she said, the realization slamming into her. "You've been watching me this whole time."

Theo's jaw tightened, but he didn't deny it.

"Who are you?" she whispered, her grip tightening on the violin case.

"I'm here to help you," he said, his voice calm but strained. "That hasn't changed."

Olivia's heart raced. She wanted to believe him, but the weight of his secrets pressed down on her. But time was running out, and if she made it out alive, she would have to deal with Theo later.

Taking a deep breath, Olivia opened the violin case. The instrument gleamed faintly in the dark, its surface dark and polished, and the strings humming with a power that felt alive. She lifted the violin carefully, her hands trembling as she tucked it beneath her chin. The bow felt heavy in her grip, as though the violin resisted her touch.

"Olivia, you don't have to do this," Theo said, stepping closer.

Her gaze hardened. "I have to end this watcher."

She drew the bow across the strings, and the first note, low and resonant, reverberated through the chamber The runes brightened, their light casting jagged shadows across the walls The ground beneath her feet trembled, and the air crackled with energy.

As the melody unfolded, the pit seemed to come alive, its darkness rising like smoke. The whispers grew louder, their language incomprehensible but filled with an urgency that tightened Olivia's chest. Each note felt like a thread unraveling inside her, pulling her closer to the edge.

As the last note lingered in the air, Olivia lowered the violin, her chest heaving. The pit roared, a soundless cry that shook the chamber.

"Olivia!" Theo shouted, his voice filled with panic.

She turned to him, tears streaming down her face. "I can't let this happen."

With a sudden surge of determination, she gripped the violin tightly and raised it above her head.

"What are you doing?" Marek demanded, stepping forward.

"Ending this," she said, her voice steady despite the fear coursing through her.

The violin hummed violently, its resistance almost unbearable. The runes flared, and the darkness surged upward, screaming in protest.

"Olivia, wait!" Theo's voice cracked, his hand outstretched.

But she didn't hesitate. She brought the violin down against the pedestal with every ounce of strength she had.

The sound of the violin shattering was deafening, a discordant note echoing through the chamber. The runes flickered and died, plunging the room into darkness.

The pit roared, its darkness rising higher before collapsing inward, pulling everything. Olivia felt the pull, her body weightless as the world around her unraveled.

"Olivia!" Theo's voice was distant, muffled.

She turned to him one last time, her heart breaking at the anguish on his face. And then, the darkness consumed her.

The chamber fell into a heavy silence. The pit was gone, its power sealed once more. Theo stood motionless, his gaze fixed on the shattered remains of the violin at his feet. Slowly, his fingers brushed against the pendant around his neck, the hourglass that had long measured the weight of faith. T.

His expression darkened. With a voice barely above a whisper, yet heavy with finality, he murmured: "Another lost soul, claimed by the abyss…bound to serve the master in the depths of darkness."

He reached into his pocket and pulled out the coin, turning it between his fingers briefly before handing it to Marek without a word. Then, without looking back, he disappeared up the stone staircase, his figure swallowed by the lingering shadows.

And, as the final echoes of the violin's unfinished melody hung in the air, it remained…a haunting reminder that nothing ever truly ends.

EPILOGUE
THE ETERNAL RESTORER

The workbench was quiet now, the tools laid out in perfect order under the warm light of a single desk lamp. Theo Callahan sat in the dim silence of his shop, the shattered remnants of the violin spread before him like pieces of a long-forgotten puzzle. His hands worked methodically, instinctively, each movement precise and deliberate.

Around his neck, the hourglass pendant hung heavy, its crimson liquid dripping again at a maddeningly slow pace. It was almost empty now.

The violin shards gleamed faintly; Theo knew it was time to start over.

The air in the shop was thick with the scent of varnish and aged wood. Theo's fingers brushed over the violin's fractured body, feeling the faint pulse of its essence—alive, restless, yearning to be whole again. The violin was as much a prisoner as he was, both bound by grandmother Destiny.

He had followed it for centuries, repairing it after every destruction, watching as new hands were drawn to its cursed melody. He had seen empires rise and fall, and generations come and go, but the violin remained constant, a relentless force that could not be silenced.

And now, Olivia had taken her place among the cursed.

He paused, the weight of the hourglass pressing against his chest. Memories of Olivia flashed through his mind: the way she had fought to resist the violin's pull, the defiance in her eyes as she raised it over her head, the heartbreak etched on her face as she sacrificed herself to save the world from darkness.

But the violin's destruction was always temporary.

Theo let out a slow breath, his fingers tightening around a delicate carving tool. He was both the Watcher and the Restorer, the one chosen to keep the cycle alive and ensure that the violin always found its way back into the world.

The shards began to hum softly as he worked, their edges fusing under his practiced touch. The runes etched into the wood glowed faintly, their intricate patterns reforming as though guided by an unseen hand. Theo didn't need to understand the runes' meaning; he only needed to bring them back.

As he placed the final piece into the violin's body, the hum grew louder, resonating through the shop like a low, mournful note. Theo set down his tools and leaned back, watching as the violin reassembled itself with an eerie grace. The last of the crimson liquid in his pendant dripped into the lower chamber, signaling the completion of his work. The violin was whole again.

Theo stared at the instrument, his expression unreadable. It rested on the workbench, its dark surface gleaming as though it had never been touched by time or destruction. The melody it carried was silent now, waiting for the next soul foolish enough to play it.

A faint knock echoed through the shop. Theo froze, his heart tightening. Slowly, he turned toward the door, where the silhouette of a woman stood, her face obscured by the shadows of the night. For a moment, Theo thought he saw Olivia.

But when the door creaked open, it wasn't her. It was someone new, a young man clutching a violin case with trembling hands, his wide eyes darting nervously around the shop.

"I was told you could help me," the man said, his voice shaking. "There's something wrong with my violin."

Theo's gaze flicked to the case, and a faint, humorless smile tugged at the corner of his lips. "Let me see what we're working with," he said quietly.

The violin on the workbench seemed to hum in anticipation, its dark, cursed melody ready to begin anew.

And so, the cycle continued.

A NOTE FROM THE AUTHOR

Dear Reader,

Thank you for taking this journey with me through The Violin's Curse. I hope the story lingered in your mind like an unfinished, haunting, and unforgettable melody. Writing this book was a labor of love, and knowing that you spent your time in its world means more than I can express.

If you liked the book, please consider leaving a review on Amazon. Your thoughts help other readers discover the story and support independent authors like me in continuing to create. Even a few words make a world of difference!

If you're interested in the deeper mysteries surrounding Theo and Thebes, including their origins and the hidden forces at play, there's more to their story waiting for you. A sequel short story revealing the truths of their past is available. To receive it, simply leave a kind review on Amazon and then reach out to me at lydialagaauthor@gmail.com, and I'll send it your way.

Thank you again for reading. Until our paths cross again in the next tale...

With gratitude,

Lydia Laga
Author

www.ingramcontent.com/pod-product-compliance
Lightning Source LLC
Chambersburg PA
CBHW061125100726
47911CB00013B/690